Anita stood outside the door marked 'Director of Surgery'. There were butterflies flapping around in her stomach.

As the door opened she raised her eyes to the tall, dark stranger. Only he wasn't a stranger. Even with the greying hair at his temples, it was unmistakably the last man in the world she'd expected to see...

'Dan!' His name escaped her lips in a hoarse whisper.

She watched the expression of disbelief in his brown eyes as he stared down at her.

He lifted his arms from his sides, took a step forward, as if he was going to wrap those firm, muscular arms around her as he'd done so often in that far-off life they'd shared together before events had forced them apart. But then he steadied himself, as if remembering all that had passed between them. He moved back, simply holding out one hand to take hers in his.

'Anita,' he said, his voice sexily husky. He pulled himself back to the present as he tried to push innumerable questions from his mind—because he knew he had to remain totally professional...

Dear Reader

I've set THE FATHERHOOD MIRACLE in Southern India, where my husband and I spent several wonderful winter holidays. The people are kind and welcoming, and the weather is sunny and warm—perfect for swimming or simply lazing on a tropical beach. We both fell in love with the place.

This story came to me when we were enjoying a fabulous holiday there. I told my husband the outline and, as always, he had some helpful input to make. Shortly after I started writing it he was diagnosed with cancer. I stopped writing to take care of him, but although he fought bravely for six months, he died. After a break, I've now finished the book, as I know he would have wanted.

Writing has proved very therapeutic for me. Although I've lost my own hero, my life is very fulfilling as a writer of romantic novels. This is my 56th book for Mills and Boon, and I've enjoyed writing each one. It's exciting that it will be published in the year that Mills and Boon celebrates its 100th birthday. All the stories I've written have been very special to me. Each one is my baby—when I'm writing it! But, like a good mother, I transfer some of my affections to the next baby that comes along to join the happy family.

I used to tell my husband that all my gorgeous heroes had some of his qualities, and Dan in THE FATHERHOOD MIRACLE is no different. I adore him, and hope you will too! My heroine, Anita, has always loved Dan, but there are many obstacles to overcome before they can be truly together. I hope you'll enjoy reading this as much as I enjoyed writing it.

With my best wishes

Margaret

THE FATHERHOOD MIRACLE

BY
MARGARET BARKER

Ⓖ™ MILLS & BOON®
Pure reading pleasure™

First published in Great Britain 2008
Large Print edition 2008
Harlequin Mills & Boon Limited,
Eton House, 18-24 Paradise Road,
Richmond, Surrey TW9 1SR

© Margaret Barker 2008

ISBN: 978 0 263 19997 0

Set in Times Roman 16½ on 19 pt.
17-1208-50340

Printed and bound in Great Britain
by Antony Rowe Ltd, Chippenham, Wiltshire

Margaret Barker has enjoyed a variety of interesting careers. A State Registered Nurse and qualified teacher, she holds a degree in French and Linguistics and is a Licentiate of the Royal Academy of Music. As a full-time writer, Margaret says, 'Writing is my most interesting career, because it fits perfectly into family life. Sadly, my husband died of cancer in 2006, but I still live in our idyllic sixteenth-century house near the East Anglian coast. Our grown-up children have flown the nest, but they often fly back again, bringing their own young families with them for wonderful weekend and holiday reunions.'

Margaret Barker has written over 50 books for Mills & Boon Medical™ Romance!

I would like to dedicate
THE FATHERHOOD MIRACLE
to my late husband, John, whose qualities
always helped to give me the essence of my
gorgeous heroes. I discussed this story with
him before he died, and, as always,
he helped to inspire me.

CHAPTER ONE

As SHE walked down the steps from the plane Anita felt the warm air wrap around her. So different to the cold, damp English winter she'd left behind. This was the kind of winter she'd enjoyed as a child. She was coming home. Except there was no one to meet her now.

She stepped out onto the tarmac, avoiding the squashy bits that were melting to the constituency of chewing gum in the late morning sun. The heat was exactly as she remembered on that day when she'd arrived back from staying with her grandmother in England, holding tightly to her amah's hand, looking across expectantly to the airport buildings, waiting for her parents to hurry out to meet them. Only then Bhanu told her very quietly that they were going back to the house by themselves.

Anita had sensed there had been something Bhanu hadn't been telling her. There had had to be because her kind, always helpful nanny had turned her head away and spoken in a strange, stilted voice, not the warm, confident tone she'd always used. The poignant memories flooded back as she walked into the Arrivals area. It was slightly cooler in here but the air-conditioning didn't seem very efficient. She pulled a moistened wet wipe from her bag and ran it over her forehead. Ah…that was better!

'Are you feeling all right, madam?'

Anita came back to the present as the man at passport control checked her passport. His eyes were quizzical as he glanced from her photograph to scrutinise her face.

She took a deep breath. 'I'm fine.'

The man smiled, displaying perfect white teeth in his friendly brown face.

'You will soon get used to the heat,' he said in the musically lilting accent she loved so much because it told her she was home again.

He reminded her vividly of a patient of her

father's who had been so grateful because her father had operated on his little daughter and saved her life that he'd turned up at the house every few days, bringing a small basket of eggs.

'A gift for your own beautiful daughter from the daughter you saved, Doctor,' he'd always said.

She smiled back at the friendly man. 'The heat doesn't worry me. I was born here in Rangalore.'

'Ah, yes.' He nodded in agreement as he turned the page and noted her date and place of birth. He checked further. 'I see you are coming to work here, Dr Sutherland. I hope you will be very happy here.'

'Thank you. I'm sure I will be.' Anita retrieved her passport.

She spoke with a conviction that was slightly forced. Over the last few years she'd learned that you made your own happiness wherever you lived. Surroundings didn't matter. You worked hard, played hard and tried not to care too much about whether you were happy. Being fulfilled was the most important part of her life. And she was fulfilled, wasn't she? Well, almost…There were certain goals beyond her reach but, then, nothing in life was perfect.

Outside the airport she climbed into one of the black and yellow taxis. The traffic was infinitely worse than it had been when she'd been a child. She thought back to the idyllic times when her parents had been alive, before she'd been taken to England and placed in an English boarding school, spending her holidays with her grand-mother. In those far-off days it had been possible to go on shopping trips in down town Rangalore in the family car, sedately cruising along the tree-lined avenues at a steady pace, sticking her little head out of the window to watch the bicycles, the men driving their cattle to the open-air market and the occasional rickshaw.

An auto rickshaw now sneaked between her taxi and a large lorry. Somewhere in front of them the traffic ground to a halt. Apart from the cow that had meandered across the road, weaving its way through the vehicles, the colour-ful scene reminded her of the traffic jam she'd endured yesterday on the M25 near Heathrow where she'd had to wait patiently whilst worrying that she would miss her plane.

And she really hadn't wanted to miss that plane. Because the doubts about what she'd been doing would have plagued her still further. She found it so hard to be positive and stop looking into the past. The time was ripe to make a new start, to put the past behind her.

The taxi edged its way forward and suddenly they were moving quickly again. Minutes later she could see the new hospital, bright and shiny in the morning sunlight. She'd been sent pictures of it along with the application form she'd filled in before her interview in London. It was a very impressive-looking building.

She felt a surge of nostalgia as she passed the old Rangalore hospital which still existed alongside the new one. It looked as if it was still in use as part of the new hospital. In her mind's eye she imagined she could see her father, stethoscope dangling around his neck, hurrying down the old hospital corridors to see some anxious patient in one of the wards or making his way to the operating theatre.

She sighed audibly. Her far-off childhood had been a happy one. She knew she couldn't re-create that by coming back here. Neither did she want to. But a complete change of surroundings from her life in England had been a good idea under the circumstances.

She looked out of the open window at the tall casuarina trees shading the wide gateway as the taxi drove up to the front of the hospital. There had been some trees in her childhood garden, she remembered. And palm trees like the ones at the edge of the car park. A man had come every evening, climbing up them with a rope around his waist which her mother had told her was to make sure that he didn't fall. She used to love to watch him shinning up the trees, tapping them and returning to the ground with the palm oil he'd siphoned off into a wooden gourd strapped around his back.

In fact, now she looked more closely, this would be the area where the garden of her old house had been! She'd heard a few years ago that some of the buildings near the old hospital had been pulled down to make way for the new hospital. So she really had come home at last!

As she paid the driver, peeling off the necessary rupees from her wallet, she tried to ignore the jet-lag enveloping her. She'd slept for a few hours on the plane and woken up refreshed. Then the excitement of being back in Rangalore had boosted her flagging energy. She knew she'd have to keep going until she was settled into her new quarters.

The porter lifted the suitcase from her and directed her to the main reception area.

Yes, she was expected, the receptionist told her. The porter would take her case to her rooms in the resident doctors' annexe. Another porter was on hand to take her to see the director of surgery, who was also in charge of Accident and Emergency.

She asked if she could freshen up before she met the director and was told that he always met up with new doctors when they arrived and was an extremely busy man who wouldn't have time to see her later.

Better go with the flow. She mustn't upset the boss's routine. All terribly efficient, she thought as she made her way along the white-painted corridor. She wondered, fleetingly, what her father would have made of this high-tech new building. Would he have felt a bit intimidated, as she did now? No, probably not. Nothing had fazed the highly regarded Richard Smith. Entirely devoted to his hospital work, his surroundings hadn't mattered.

The porter had now disappeared, having pointed her in the right direction. As she stood outside the door marked 'Director of Surgery', there were butterflies flapping around in her stomach.

She felt like a child on her first day at school rather than a qualified, experienced doctor. Which she was, she reminded herself to try and boost her confidence. Oh, well, here goes... Deep breath...

She knocked and waited.

Several moments passed. Should she knock

again? Perhaps he was on the phone… No, better to wait… Don't antagonise… Oh, my God! As the door opened she raised her eyes to the tall, dark stranger. Only he wasn't a stranger. Even with the greying hair on his temples, it was un-mistakably the last man in the world she'd expected to see…

'Dan!' His name escaped her lips in a hoarse whisper.

She watched the expression of disbelief in his brown eyes as he stared down at her. He ran his tongue around his lips… Oh, God, those sexy lips that had driven her to distraction…and still would if ever…but that would never happen.

He lifted his arms from his sides, took a step forward as if he was going to wrap those firm, muscular arms around her as he'd done so often in that far-off life back in London that they'd shared together before events had forced them apart. But then he steadied himself, as if remem-bering all that had passed between them. He moved back, simply holding out one hand to take hers in his.

'Anita,' he said, his voice sexily husky. 'Where on earth have you sprung from?'

'I was told you were expecting me. I've been appointed to the new post in Accident and Emergency.'

His brow wrinkled. Moments of suspense passed before light seemed to dawn in his eyes. He breathed out in an audible sigh.

'The notes on my desk say Dr A. M. Sutherland so…'

'I changed from Anita Margaret Smith when I married Dr Mark Sutherland.'

He glanced up briefly, wanting so much to quiz her about her marriage. 'Of course, I had heard that you'd married.' It had happened about a year after they'd parted, he remembered. And he hadn't seen her since that fateful day when he'd taken her back to her flat, both of them agonising over the decisions they'd had to make after their long emotional discussion that evening. They had been planning to take some time out and then get together for another discussion when they next met, tell each other what they'd decided.

But he'd known as he'd left her the only honourable option he had to make. He'd loved her too much to put her through a childless marriage. Her happiness had been the most important thing he had to make sure of. Oh, they'd discussed adoption and donor insemination that evening but he'd sensed by her reaction that it hadn't been what she'd wanted, and she'd deserved to have a child of her own. So he'd had to be strong, he'd had to be the one to end their relationship and give her the freedom to find someone else who could give her the family she so longed for.

He pulled himself back to the present as the questions poured into his mind. Was it a good marriage? Was her husband with her? He tried to push the questions from his mind because he knew he had to remain totally professional. The agency had said Dr Sutherland was the best candidate. The fact that she was married was irrelevant—except that it meant she was off limits as far as a meaningful personal relationship with her was concerned. That was the thing he must remember. There was no going back to the past and…

He took a deep breath as he tried to concentrate on the details in front of him. 'To be honest, your notes have only just arrived on my desk. My secretary told me the London agency had appointed the best candidate and I've always trusted their judgement.'

He swallowed hard, as if struggling to come to terms with the new situation that had threatened to shatter his composure. 'You're earlier than I expected.'

'Yes, the plane was early and I went through passport control quickly.'

'Good, good,' Dan said distractedly, as he ran a hand through his dark hair.

Anita noticed that Dan's hair was still thick and the streaks of steel grey made him even more handsome, which didn't help her to still her churning emotions. She'd accepted his rejection all those years ago so she must try to look at him without comparing him with the wonderful lover she'd known what now seemed to be a lifetime ago. She'd forced herself to accept that Dan had made it clear in the letter he'd sent her that he wanted to end their affair, so it would be stupid to rake over the coals.

Dan cleared his throat. 'You'd better come in.'

'Thank you.'

She must keep this interview formal, professional and above all she mustn't let him know how he'd broken her heart. She'd stuck it back together over and over again and she wasn't going to allow him to affect her emotionally in any way. She sat down in the chair he'd indicated before resuming his place behind the large desk. He seemed nervous all of a sudden, as well he might be. It was an impossible situation, being confronted by a rejected lover. If she'd had any idea that this was going to happen, she would have…

'Well, this is unexpected,' Dan said, his piercing brown eyes holding hers.

'For me, too. I had no idea you were working in Rangalore. I thought you were still in America.'

'No, I left America to move back to India. I worked in Mumbai for a while. If you remember, I was born there.'

'Yes, I remember when we first met we were

both surprised to find that we were both born in India.'

Don't think about that day when they'd first met, she told herself quickly. Don't allow yourself to remember the heady experience of love at first sight—because that's what it had been. Looking up at the platform in the lecture theatre at medical school, trying to concentrate on what this fabulously intriguing man was saying when all the time her heart was thumping with a compelling attraction. And afterwards, when she'd approached him and asked a question about something he'd said in the lecture and he'd suggested that they go out for a coffee together so that he could explain more fully.

She leaned back against the leather-covered chair, breathing deeply to steady herself. It had been a lifetime ago when they'd sat in that London coffee-bar, swapping stories and experiences, finding they had so much in common, revelling in the electric current of mutual attraction that had sparked between them.

'We both said we'd always planned to return to India,' he said quietly.

'Yes.' She hesitated. 'India has a way of drawing you back. Rangalore was where I spent my childhood. But you were born in Mumbai. What made you come to work here in the south?'

'Oh, the climate is so much easier for my…for working and living in,' he finished quickly. He couldn't divulge the real reason…she couldn't possibly understand.

She swallowed hard. He was staring at her quizzically. She longed to tell him that she was a widow, that her feelings had never changed even though he'd rejected her, but she'd come out to India to start a new life, not to resurrect an old one—even if that were possible.

She glanced around at the director's opulent office with its leather chairs, the large, highly polished desk, the book-lined walls, the large picture window overlooking the hospital gardens, all the trappings of a successful surgeon. It was obvious to her that Dan was still a highly ambitious, powerful man. But she'd also thought he would be a wonderful family man as well. Their relationship had seemed to be heading towards a state of permanency when she'd divulged how much she would love to have children. She remembered how awful it had been when Dan had told her he'd had a vasectomy. He'd said that since he'd met her he'd sought out specialists' opinions as to whether a reversal would be possible. But they'd told him after examination that a reversal would be impossible in his case because of complications during the original operation.

She remembered the long, agonising discussion that evening, how they'd talked about the possibility of adoption or donor insemination, which had seemed the only option. She remembered struggling with the disappointment of learning that she could never have the child of the man she loved. They'd agreed to take time out while they sorted out their feelings and decided what they were going to do. He'd taken her back to her own flat—she'd been living in Dan's flat most of the time, she remembered.

And then, the very next day, had come the bombshell. He'd delivered her a letter by hand but hadn't even rung the bell or phoned her or given her any possibility of contacting him.

He was leaving London immediately to take up a hospital post in America. She remembered vividly his words in the letter where he'd told her that he thought it was best, in the circumstances, if 'we end our relationship. That way nobody will get hurt.'

Nobody will get hurt! She'd been devastated! He may as well have taken a scalpel to her heart and removed it completely.

She took a deep breath as the memories flooded back and somehow she managed to remain silent, clasping her hands together so that she could concentrate on looking composed, even if she didn't feel it.

Dan was also regaining his composure. He'd learned to put Anita out of his mind over the years. But here she was in the flesh, bringing the past so poignantly back to him, looking so infinitely desirable, so sexy, so beautiful. Even though she'd just made a long-haul flight she looked calm and relaxed. Her cream-coloured lightweight cotton jacket and skirt looked cool as they clung to the curves of her slim body. He could see the swell of her breasts moving as she breathed.

Mmm…he could feel the stirrings of desire deep down in his body as he remembered how it felt to hold her in his arms. His feelings for her hadn't changed a bit. But once again he chided himself for forgetting she was now married. The past was over between them.

He gave himself a mental shake. He'd better pull himself together. When he'd got over the shock he would work out how he was going to handle this. Anita was a married woman, end of story. He didn't tangle with married women. And he had his own family commitments now…

The phone was ringing.

'Dan Mackintosh.' He listened with growing concern. 'I'm on my way, Sister. Yes, pull in as many extra staff as you can.'

He put the phone down and stood up. 'Red

alert in A and E. Major traffic accident on the Rangalore ring road. I'll have to go.'

He was opening the door, holding it back for her.

She sprang to her feet. 'Would you like me to help?'

'Aren't you tired after the journey?'

'Not any more. I think the adrenaline always kicks in when there's an emergency, doesn't it?'

'We could certainly use another experienced A and E doctor.' He was looking down at her, seemingly weighing up the pros and cons of throwing Anita in at the deep end. 'OK, let's go.'

She felt his hand briefly on the back of her waist, guiding her along the corridor. She deliberately focussed her mind on the task in hand. The emergency work she would have to deal with would help to get her back on an emotionally even keel.

The first casualties were being wheeled into the A and E reception area as Anita and Dan arrived. The first patient she treated was in obvious pain. She checked with the paramedic escorting the woman, who was lying flat on the trolley. Mild sedation had been given at the scene of the accident. Anita reinforced this before checking on the injuries. The paramedic, very wisely, had strapped the woman to a backboard.

Anita leaned over her patient, speaking in English, relieved to find that the woman understood her. The woman told her that her name was Ayesha and she was twenty-five. Her neck was where she was feeling most pain. When the crash had happened she had been propelled forward onto the air bag and had felt a distinct clicking in her neck.

Anita made her patient as comfortable as she could whilst arranging for a nurse to take Ayesha to X-Ray. She had to move on immediately to a young English woman who was crying loudly for help.

'Nobody's listening to me,' the woman wailed as she grabbed Anita's hand. 'My baby's due next month and I've had terrible backache since they pulled me out of the car. It was burning, you see, and so they had to get me out quickly. One of the volunteers lifted me up into the ambulance and I felt this awful pain.'

The patient's name was Jane. Anita transferred her to a cubicle where she could give her a gynaecological examination. As she scrubbed up and put on some sterile gloves the patient continued to chatter nervously to her.

'I don't want to miscarry, Doctor. You've really got to save this baby because my husband and I have waited so long. We've been trying for a family and when I found I was pregnant I was over the moon.'

Anita examined her patient carefully. As she peeled off her gloves at the end of the examination Dan came into the cubicle.

'Everything OK in here?'

She drew him to one side. 'Thirty-seven week pregnancy. Patient is in labour,' she said quietly. 'The cervix is almost fully dilated. We'll have to move quickly if—'

'I'll transfer her to our emergency obstetrics department as soon as—'

'Ah-h-h!' The patient screamed as she grabbed

Anita's arm. 'Don't leave me, Doctor. The baby's coming, it's coming, it's—'

'Don't push yet, Jane,' Dan said, taking control of the situation as he signalled to a nurse to bring over the Entonox machine. Seconds later he was holding the gas and air mask over their patient's face.

'Breathe into the mask, steady rhythmic breathing, steadily…good, good…'

Anita checked and could see that Jane was now fully dilated. She told Dan that Jane could start pushing on the next contraction.

It was one of the swiftest births that Anita had ever assisted at. Afterwards, as she cradled the slippery baby boy in her arms, she looked up at Dan and smiled. He smiled down at her, that heart-rending smile that at one time had driven her crazy with desire.

'Phew!' he said, under his breath. 'That was a close one.'

She nodded, thinking of her heightened anxiety as she'd seen the cord looped around the baby's neck. She'd had only seconds to disentangle it before the baby had rushed down the birth canal.

Dan put his hand on her arm. 'Thanks, Anita. You certainly haven't lost your touch where deliveries are concerned. You were always good with babies.'

'I love babies,' she said.

'Yes, I remember,' he said huskily as he turned away and began busying himself with the array of instruments at the side of the trolley. 'Time to get this one to Obstetrics so they can start on the postnatal checks.'

'After baby's had a cuddle from his mother,' Anita said firmly, placing the newborn boy in his mother's arms.

The tiny, crumpled face had stopped screaming as the baby lay curled up against his mother.

'Thank you so much, Doctor,' Jane said as she kissed her baby's forehead. 'You were all wonderful. Has my husband arrived yet?'

Anita patted her patient's hand. 'He's on his way. Nurse called him on your mobile. He's held up in the tailback of the traffic jam caused when that lorry ploughed through the central reservation. He'll be here as soon as things start moving again.'

Jane sighed happily. 'He'll be so thrilled. He wanted a boy. I just wanted a healthy baby. We'd been trying for so long—he is healthy, isn't he, Doctor?'

Anita smiled reassuringly. 'All the signs are good so far. We're transferring you both to our obstetrics department for your postnatal checks.'

A look of concern crossed the mother's face. 'But you're going to come with me, aren't you, Doctor?'

'You'll be in good hands, Jane. I'll come along as soon as I can get away from here. There are still a number of patients to be seen and…'

Dan had hurried over to her side, his hand lightly touching the small of her back. 'Anita, go with Jane to Obstetrics, settle her in there and then go off duty—in fact, you're not yet officially on duty. I don't want jet-lag catching up on you. Two emergency doctors have just arrived. So when you've settled Jane go off and get some rest. I'll phone you this evening with instructions for tomorrow.'

Anita stretched her legs under the sheet and looked up at the unfamiliar ceiling. The phone by the bed was ringing and she couldn't think where on earth she was. The last snooze she'd had was on a plane so...

Automatically, she picked up the phone and managed a croaky whisper.

'Anita, is that you?'

She tried to clear her throat. 'I think so.'

She recognised his voice immediately as memories of the immediate past rushed back. She'd done some work in A and E, taken a patient to Obstetrics, been shown to her room in the doctors' quarters and crashed out. She could see her clothes strewn over a chair nearby.

'Sorry to wake you up but I thought it best to try and put you onto Rangalore time as soon as possible. Do you feel like coming out for supper with me?'

'Now?'

Dan's throaty chuckle came down the phone. 'You've got to eat, you know.'

'Yes, but you just mentioned supper…it feels more like breakfast-time.'

'I'm sure we could find you some bacon and eggs somewhere. I need to brief you about tomorrow.'

'OK.' She was wide awake now. Glancing at the clock on her bedside table, she saw it was seven o'clock. Through the window the last remnants of twilight hung over the roofs of the hospital buildings.

'Meet me in Reception, say, eight o'clock?'

She agreed and put the phone down quickly. Talking to Dan was difficult, to put it mildly, having had no contact with him since the night he'd taken her home after their soul-destroying discussion. And then receiving his letter, which had left her with a feeling of complete futility. It had been as if everything worthwhile in her life had ended, that she'd had nothing else to live for. There had been nothing but an empty feeling of rejection, of complete disillusionment.

And here she was agreeing to go out and have supper with the man who'd shattered all her illusions of happiness. The man who'd been responsible for the nights she'd lain awake, longing for the oblivion that only sleep gave her when it finally and elusively claimed her.

As she climbed out of bed she told herself she must be mad to even think she could go out anywhere with Dan. But he was, after all, her boss now so she couldn't have said no. Part of her...a big part of her...was actually looking forward to seeing him, even though this whole situation of working with him again was fraught with complications.

She dragged her suitcase across the floor and plonked it on top of the ruffled sheet. She winced as she switched on the main light and the brightness hit her sleep-soaked eyes. Oh, dear, she hadn't escaped the dreaded jet-lag by taking a few hours' sleep. She'd simply postponed it.

Dan put down the phone and lay back against the sofa cushions in his sitting room. The air-conditioning was comforting after his long day at the hospital. He'd showered and changed as soon as he'd got home.

He heard the sound of the front door opening and moments later a mini-whirlwind charged into the room.

'Daddy, Daddy!' The small boy flung himself into his arms. 'We had supper on the beach. It was a picnic. Lots of my friends and their mummies and daddies and some of their amahs were there. It was Tim's birthday. He was six—that's what I'll be next birthday, won't I? I thought you might come.'

Samaya, Joshua's amah, removed a speck of sand from her silk sarong as she smiled down at her charge. 'Daddy was busy at the hospital, Joshua. I told you he—'

'I tried to get away but it wasn't possible,' Dan said, holding his precious son close to him as a pang of guilt shot through him. When he was working at the hospital he managed to concentrate on what he was doing. But when he was home with Josh he worried that as a working father he was neglecting him.

'Tell you what we'll do,' he said, shifting his son onto his knee. 'We'll go to the beach on Sunday. I'll take a whole day off and we'll go swimming and play games.'

'Yes, yes!' Josh was clapping his hands together, grinning broadly at the prospect of a whole day with his father. 'You promise, Daddy, don't you?'

Dan promised. He couldn't back down now. He never broke a promise, did he?

Well, not intentionally. He thought fleetingly about Anita. As soon as she'd told him the one thing he'd dreaded—that she wanted a family— he'd known that the only honest option had been to tell her about the vasectomy he'd had. He'd already checked out whether this could be reversed. But, as the specialist had confirmed once more that this wouldn't be possible, he'd known he would have to discuss it with Anita. He couldn't have led her on, pretending that all was well.

Dan scooped up his son and carried him upstairs, calling over his shoulder to tell Samaya that he would give Joshua his bath, put him to bed and read his story.

It wasn't just guilt that was driving him on that night to try to be a good father. It was nerves about the way he was going to handle the coming encounter with Anita. Was he mad to invite her out now, knowing nothing about her life in the intervening years? And how was he to tell her that he was now, miraculously a father.

As he hugged his little boy against his chest he told himself that he could simply have called her into his office tomorrow morning and briefed her about what she was expected to do in the hospital. But, no, he'd chosen to take the bull by the horns and find out everything he could about her…and especially about her marriage.

CHAPTER TWO

ANITA was feeling decidedly nervous as she walked into Reception. She'd taken care to choose a simple, casual outfit, dove-grey trousers with a pale blue button-up shirt—something that didn't look as if she'd tried too hard. Because the last thing she wanted Dan to think was that he could just whistle and she would come running. His rejection of her had affected her deeply. She was remembering now how, initially, it had changed her personality. She'd felt as if she'd lost herself, as if she hadn't known who she was any more.

Her work hadn't suffered at the hospital because her intense medical training had meant she'd been able to perform like a professional, putting her emotional turmoil on hold while on duty. But off duty she had felt her usually strong personality, her ability to cope with everyday life, draining away from her. The real world had been something she hadn't been able to handle any more. That had been one reason why her platonic relationship with Mark had been so comforting. Mark had been full of common sense. He'd kept her feet on the ground—made her go out, go through the motions that she was actually enjoying herself, even though her heart hadn't been in the social situations she'd found herself in.

Walking into the crowded reception now, she wondered now if she should keep up the pretence that she still had a husband, at least until the boundaries of their relationship had been firmly established.

As she glanced towards the front entrance to the hospital she felt a hand on her arm. A feeling of nostalgia swam over her as she detected the faint scent of Dan's aftershave. She mustn't give in to nostalgia!

'Glad you could make it,' he said evenly. 'I thought you might have gone back to sleep.'

She looked up and the years between seemed to slip away. She caught her breath as she thought what a handsome man he was.

'I've unpacked, had to find something to wear.'

'You look most attractive, from where I'm standing.'

She flinched and he noticed.

'I'm allowed to compliment a woman on her appearance, even if she is married, aren't I?'

She didn't reply as she began to move to the outside door. He was right behind her in the crush of people trying to get in and out, all intent on their own business. She breathed a sigh of relief as she reached the other side of the main door. The evening warmth wrapped around her and all her senses heightened. The old familiar excitement of simply being alive in this vibrant atmosphere returned. She knew she could only be in one wonderful place on earth—her beloved India.

'It's good to be back!'

He smiled down at her. 'I'm glad you think so. I've booked a table in downtown Rangalore at Marcel's so we'll need to take a taxi.'

'Marcel's? Is it a European restaurant?'

'The owner is an interesting man from Goa whose ancestors were Portuguese so the cuisine is a mixture of Indian and European. I think you'll like it.'

They reached the kerb. A bullock cart was ambling past, a well-filled taxi trying unsuccessfully to overtake it. The passengers in the taxi were striving to take in the air from the open windows. A colourful piece of a sari was floating out as its owner breathed in the fumes from the surrounding traffic.

'It's going to be difficult to get a taxi. I've got my car in the hospital car park but I don't think that would be any quicker in this traffic.'

Anita pointed down the road. 'There's a *tuktuk* over there, dropping somebody off. Let's see if he'll take us.'

Dan took her arm to steady her in the crush of people as they hurried to the vehicle. He spoke to the driver before helping Anita to squeeze through the open doorway of the auto rickshaw. She leaned back against the uncomfortable seat.

Dan climbed in beside her after negotiating the price with the driver. Conversation was virtually impossible as the man set off at what seemed like an impossibly high speed, given the complex traffic conditions.

As they wove in and out of the lines of traffic, somehow managing to get round all the cars, buses and animals in between, Dan leaned nearer to ask if she was OK.

She smiled at him. 'Why shouldn't I be? It all seems perfectly normal to me.'

Dan laughed. 'I'd forgotten you were brought up here.'

She struggled to hear him amidst the deafening cacophony. 'What did you say? I missed that.'

He shook his head, still laughing. 'Doesn't matter.'

They drove on without attempting any further conversation but with a warm feeling of togetherness that Anita found to be comforting but scary at the same time. It was almost as if the intervening years hadn't happened. Here they were having a night out on the town just like they used to do. Alarm bells were ringing in her head but she chose to ignore them. Perhaps she could just pretend for a few hours and go back to reality later? It was a tempting idea but something she had to resist. A few hours of pretence would weaken her resolve.

'Here we are,' Dan shouted above the din of the engine as the driver slewed the three-wheeled *tuk-tuk* towards the pavement.

A smart Indian commissionaire dressed in a brightly coloured uniform, his head swathed in a large black turban, came forward from the door of the restaurant to greet them.

'Good evening, sir, good evening, madam. Do you have a booking for this evening or…?'

The rest of the commissionaire's words were lost in the general noise of car horns, barking dogs and loud music from a passing car. Anita was relieved to find it was quieter inside. The tall high ceilings of the old, beautifully refurbished colonial-style building helped to create a calm ambience.

She took a deep breath. The cool air of the air-conditioning was very welcome after the heat from the exposed engine of the *tuk-tuk*.

Marcel came forward to shake hands with Dan. They appeared to know each other well.

'Marcel, this is Dr Anita Sutherland, a new colleague of mine at the hospital.'

Marcel smiled broadly. 'Delighted to meet you, Dr Sutherland. If you would like to come this way, I'll show you to your table.'

Dan ordered a bottle of champagne. Without realising it, Anita frowned. They'd drunk champagne together on so many occasions when they'd been in the middle of their heady relationship. But she really didn't want him to think that by coming out to a restaurant together she was going to forget his rejection and slip back into some kind of easy relationship that would lead to more suffering for her in the end.

'You look worried. We don't have to drink it all,' Dan said defensively.

'I've heard you say that before and...' She stopped as her voice choked.

'That's what I used to say, wasn't it?' he said huskily.

She hesitated, telling herself she had to be strong. 'It's so easy...when you've known someone for a long time to forget that everything has changed,' she said, quietly.

'Not everything.' He reached across the table and placed his hand over hers. 'Some things haven't changed. You're still a young, beautiful, desirable woman.'

She withdrew her hand. 'Dan, we've got to set the parameters if we're going to work together. Otherwise...'

The waiter had arrived with the champagne, showing the label to Dan before deftly removing the cork and pouring it into the two crystal glasses.

Dan held his glass towards her. 'Here's to a good working relationship. I'm sorry if you think I overstepped the mark just now. Please, don't get me wrong. I totally respect that you're married to Mark.'

He paused and his brow furrowed. 'As a matter of interest, where is Mark at the moment?'

She took a sip of champagne, before setting it down on the starched white tablecloth. Looking across at Dan, she knew it would be no good trying to keep up the pretence that she was still a married woman. Sooner or later…

She took a deep breath. 'Mark died six months after we were married.'

She saw the deep shock register on Dan's face. He made as if to reach for her hand again but then thought better of it.

'I'm truly sorry,' he said, quietly. 'I had no idea. Was it…?'

'He was killed in a climbing accident in the Lake District.'

'That must have been very hard for you,' Dan said genuinely concerned.

'Yes,' she said, softly. 'Yes, it was…'

Her voice choked again. She couldn't begin to describe her feelings during the immediate years after her husband's death. Mark had known she hadn't loved him in the way she'd loved Dan. He'd been a true friend and when he'd comforted her after Dan's rejection she'd become very fond of him. When he'd asked her to marry him, telling her that his love was enough for the two of them, she'd agreed because she'd known it would make him happy and she hadn't wanted to lose him. He'd been the one stable factor in her emotional life. She'd respected him enormously and she'd hoped she would learn to love him.

But she never did, or at least not in the way she had loved Dan. She had respected Mark enormously, put all her energies into trying to reciprocate his love. But try as she would, the spectre of Dan had always been somewhere in the background of her consciousness.

She gave an involuntary sigh.

'Are you OK?' Dan's eyes revealed his concern.

'I…I was just reliving the past. Yes, it was very hard for me to come to terms with…with everything. One day Mark was there, packing his rucksack to go off for the weekend with his climbing friends…and the next day I was a widow, collecting his rucksack from the hospital.'

The waiter had arrived and was waiting patiently to take their order. Anita looked across the table at Dan. The depth of emotion she was feeling had temporarily removed her appetite.

'Why don't you choose for both of us?' she said quietly. 'You know—'

She broke off in mid-sentence. She'd been going to say that he knew what she liked but that again was because she was slipping too easily into the easy rapport they'd shared, and that kind of relationship must never be re-created. A man who could break her heart with his rejection, as Dan had done, was not to be trusted ever again.

'Actually, I've changed my mind because I'd like to have curry on my first night back in India,' she said firmly. 'I particularly like Madras chicken.'

'A good choice,' Dan said. 'I'll join you and we could mix and share several items. You like grated coconut, I remember, and we'll have some chicken Jalfrezi with some spicy lime pickle, don't you think? I'll get some fried rice for you and I'll have some plain boiled rice. And how about some popadums? They're called papads here. That always used to get your digestive juices flowing when we lived in London.'

The years had rolled away again and Anita felt as if she was back in that little Indian restaurant just down the road from the London hospital where Dan had been a surgeon and she had been working towards her final medical exams. How was she ever to keep to a platonic professional relationship with Dan when he seemed to have slipped so easily into the easygoing relationship they'd always enjoyed?

As the waiter went away with their order she took another sip of her champagne and raised her eyes towards Dan. He was watching her with a look of concern on his face.

'You were telling me about Mark,' he said quietly. 'You must have needed all your strength to cope with such a traumatic situation.'

'Yes, it was tough…but the pain eased over the years.'

That wasn't really true. She still wondered if she'd made Mark as happy as she'd tried to during their six months of marriage. She'd been plagued by guilt even after he died.

When she'd first agreed to marry Mark, she'd

thrown all her energies into the business of loving him. But she'd discovered that you can't force yourself into that kind of love. Falling in love was something that happened, that hit you with such force that you couldn't ignore it. Something like the love she'd felt for Dan…and still did, if she dared to admit it. From trying desperately to love Mark, she was now in a reverse situation. Trying to ignore the love she felt for a man she couldn't possibly ever have a real relationship with again.

'Life can be very tough,' Dan said. 'But I'm glad the pain eased over the years.'

She swallowed hard. How could Dan possibly understand what she'd had to endure since he'd rejected her?

The waiter brought crisp, spicy popadums. Anita found she was hungry now as she ate the curry with all the fragrant side dishes. Looking across the table at Dan, she found herself relaxing. It really was so wonderful to be with him again, even if she had to keep reminding herself that she mustn't give him the slightest

inkling that they could re-create their past relationship—because they absolutely couldn't.

Why not? She banished the wicked little voice
inside her head. Because she couldn't bear to
have her heart broken again. What she had to
remember was that Dan hadn't changed. It was
as simple as that.

They ate ice cream after their curry, which Dan
pointed out had always helped to cool them
down again after the fiery spices. She'd given up
hope of him stopping the various references to
that former life. It was too ingrained in their
memories to be totally excluded, so why not go
with the flow? It wasn't unpleasant to her, was
it? Guiltily, she admitted to herself that she was
enjoying this brief interlude of cosy intimacy.
But she reminded herself sternly that this was as
far as it was going.

It had to stop as soon as they left the restaurant.
It was a temporary idyll which she mustn't allow
herself to take too seriously. It meant nothing to
Dan so it must be of no consequence to her.

Dan was telling the waiter they'd have their

coffee on the veranda. This was a delightful airy addition to the restaurant at the back of the building. It was open on one side with mosquito screening that allowed them to look through at the garden. Tropical plants and flowers grew out there in profusion, each area illuminated by hidden lights. Above, she could see the moon beaming down, lighting up the scenery with an ethereal white light.

As she took a sip of her coffee she remarked that they hadn't finished the champagne.

Dan grinned. 'I said we wouldn't. My intentions were totally honourable. In fact it was a medical decision I made. I simply wanted you to drink a glass or two to relax you. You were looking tired and worried when you came in, whereas now you look…'

He leaned forward and took hold of her hand. This time she allowed herself the momentary luxury of allowing their fingers to touch before she withdrew her hand and mentally reproached herself for giving in.

'Now you look almost radiant.'

'Almost?'

'Give or take a little jet-lag, I could almost imagine that—'

Dan's mobile phone was ringing. He frowned as he checked who the caller was. 'Sorry, Anita, I'll have to answer this one. Excuse me a moment.'

He got up from the table and began to move away. She distinctly heard him say, 'Yes, Samaya,' before he disappeared from her view.

Who was Samaya? A girlfriend, perhaps? She knew nothing about this present-day Dan. He may seem like the same man she'd loved and worked with but there must have been some changes over the years. How long had it been since she'd seen him?

She leaned back against the cushions of the wicker armchair as she tried to remember. It must be seven years since that awful day when she'd received his letter saying that he was going to America, that she mustn't try to contact him, that she should try to forget him, look to the future and hopefully have the family she wanted, one day. He was going to get on with his career and try to forget her.

She put down her coffee-cup. She'd been deluding herself while they'd shared their curry. She'd allowed herself to be lulled into believing that…well, what had she been believing? Something that her heart, not her head, had dictated to her.

He was coming back and the familiar pangs of longing came to her as she saw him weaving his way through the small tables on the veranda. He came round the back of her chair so that she had to turn sideways to look up at him.

'I'm sorry, Anita. Something's come up. I'll have to go home.'

Dan's mobile was ringing again. He was still clutching it in his hand. 'Yes, Samaya, I'm on my way. It will take a few minutes before the infant paracetamol takes effect. I'll be home as soon as I can get a taxi. No, don't panic. I'm coming.'

Anita was already on her feet. Many possibilities were running through her mind but the main thing was that there was some sort of crisis involving a child. Whose child? She couldn't help speculating. She felt numb. Not Dan's, surely? Dan, who'd left her without understanding how she had felt. Dan, who'd told her he couldn't father children and felt she'd be better off without him.

She took a deep breath and, summoning all her dignity, managed to walk out of the restaurant looking calm. Her legs felt shaky as she stood outside in the evening warmth with the indefinable scents wafting out from the restaurant and the dusty smells coming from the busy road.

The commissionaire whistled up a taxi from somewhere and soon they were driving through the traffic. The congestion had eased. She wanted to ask so many questions but the look on Dan's face wasn't encouraging so she remained silent.

Dan was worried, worried about the fact that Josh had a high temperature but also worried about telling Anita that he had a son.

He was remembering that last occasion when they'd been together, when he'd still thought that conceiving a child, given his medical diagnosis, had been impossible. The kindest course of action for Anita had been for him to end their relationship. To give Anita the option of finding someone who could give her the children she longed for. It had broken his heart to make the swift end to their relationship. He'd known he had to be strong for her sake and write that letter. He'd hardened his heart, knowing that he mustn't give her an inkling of hope about the situation.

He turned to look at her now in the twinkling lights from the traffic outside their taxi. She looked so beautiful, the intervening years hadn't aged her at all. But she was sitting stiffly as far away from him as she possibly could get. Had she surmised he'd got a child and didn't want to ask him about the situation? He longed to reach out and take her hand, to explain everything...but not now when he had to get home and take care of his precious Josh. Even so, he would soon have to broach the subject of why he had a son but he'd no idea how she would react when she knew the truth.

He moved nearer. 'Anita,' he said quietly, 'I have a small son who's not feeling well.'

She swallowed hard at the impossibly wounding revelation. 'I'm sorry… I mean, I'm sorry your son's not well,' she added quickly.

'You're surprised I have a son?'

'Of course I'm surprised,' she said, as lightly as she could, trying to ignore the emotional turmoil she was experiencing. 'But people change, don't they? You must have discovered it was possible for you to have a family after all.'

'No, it wasn't like that! As you know, I thought I couldn't have children because of the vasectomy I told you about but…'

He broke off, knowing this wasn't the time or the place to go into complicated explanations about the miraculous surgical intervention that had finally resolved the problem.

'Anita, I owe it to you to explain everything,' he hurried on. 'But not now. It's too long and complicated a story. There are aspects of my life that have changed and—'

'Dan, you're not making much sense. You're simply confusing me.'

'It's a long story. I'll explain soon…but not now.'

Her emotions were in turmoil but she tried hard to look calm as she shrugged her shoulders.

'Dan, it doesn't matter any more. It's all in the past. Are you married to the woman who phoned you? I heard you call her Samaya.'

'Samaya is my son's amah.'

'And your wife?'

'We're divorced. Joshua's mother lives in America.'

She remained silent as she digested the facts of this complicated situation.

Dan broke the silence moments later. 'We're near my house now but we'll go round to the hospital first so I can drop you off.'

Her professional training stepped in. 'If we're near your house, I'll come with you. The sooner you get home, the better. The driver can take me to the hospital after he's dropped you off. Alternatively, two doctors' opinions would be better than one. As we both know, a high fever can sometimes be of no consequence in a small child, but on the other hand it could be masking something critical. Children are so unpredictable.'

Dan hesitated but only for a split second. 'Thanks, Anita. I would value your opinion. Are you sure you want to?'

'Yes, I'm sure.'

The taxi was leaving the main road, turning in between wrought-iron gates. Anita looked out of the side window of the taxi as they drove up a long private drive. Dan's house looked beautiful in the lights thrown up from the sides of the gravel parking area. He was asking the driver to wait until he'd assessed whether he would need to take his child to the hospital.

They were met at the door by Samaya.

'I didn't call you again, Dan,' she said quietly, 'but Joshua vomited a few minutes ago.'

Dan took the stairs at breakneck speed. Anita followed Dan as quickly as she could. Swiftly he led the way along a broad corridor. The door to Josh's bedroom was wide open. The little boy sitting on the side of the bed smiled when he saw his father.

'I've been sick,' he said, proudly pointing to the plastic bucket at the side of his bed. 'We had chocolate cake at the party. I think I ate too much of it.'

As Dan glanced towards the brown contents of the bucket he felt relief flooding through him.

'Is that your considered opinion, Dr Joshua? The patient ate too much cake?' Dan asked his son solemnly.

Josh grinned, mischievously. 'Well, what do you think, Daddy?'

'I'll have to check you out before I commit myself. But first I want you to meet another doctor I've brought in to give me some advice on this difficult case. Josh, this is Dr Sutherland.'

Anita sat down beside Josh on the bed. 'Hi, Josh. You can call me Anita, if you like.'

Josh smiled at Anita. She smelt nice. Sort of perfumy. Usually he didn't like ladies who had a perfumy smell but this one was different.

'Are you a friend of my daddy's?'

'Yes, an old friend,' Dan said as he sat down on the other side of Josh.

Josh studied Anita. 'She doesn't look old—well, not very. How old are you, Anita?'

'I'm thirty, Josh.'

'Daddy's thirty-nine. Nearly forty, so that's really old. I'm nearly six,' Josh said proudly.

'Josh, I just need to take your temperature.'

Dan took an electronic thermometer from the medical bag that Samaya had brought him.

He took Josh's temperature then studied the result. 'It's just a flick above normal.'

'Looks as if the paracetamol acted as an emetic and lowered the temperature,' Anita said quietly.

'You're a good doctor, aren't you?' Josh said.

Anita smiled. 'You don't need a medical degree to deduce the obvious. Any mother would realise what had happened.'

'Are you a mother? Have you got children?'

'No, Josh, I was speaking generally about the mothers I meet when I'm working as a doctor.'

Josh leaned forward. 'My mother's a doctor as well as a mother but I never see her so I don't know whether she's good at finding out what's wrong with people. Do you, Daddy?'

Dan looked distinctly uncomfortable. 'I think

she's probably OK after all her training and experience. Now just roll on to your back, Josh, and let me feel your tummy.'

Dan palpated Josh's abdomen, paying special attention to the area around the appendix.

'Even though the case seems pretty obvious, I like to make sure,' he said to Anita.

'Shall I take away the bucket, Dan?' Samaya asked.

Dan nodded.

Josh sat up. 'I'm hungry, Daddy.'

'Just a sip of water to begin with, Josh, and then I think you should try and get some sleep.'

The little boy climbed onto Dan's lap. 'Will you tell me a story?'

'Yes.' Dan looked at Anita, who was already standing up.

'I'll say goodnight to both of you,' she said, looking down at the touching scene. A lump came into her throat and she swallowed hard. This was how she'd imagined life would be for her and Dan during that idyllic time when they'd meant everything to each other. Josh was the spitting image of his father. He even had the same expressive brown eyes.

Dan made as if to stand up but Anita told him to stay where he was. She would let herself out to the waiting taxi.

'I'll see you in the morning at the hospital,' Dan said. 'Perhaps you could come first to my office so I can brief you about all the details I meant to give you this evening. We didn't get around to discussing half the things I had to tell you.'

Anita smiled from the doorway and waved a hand. She didn't trust herself to try and speak.

Josh waved back as he jumped off his father's lap and ran towards Anita. 'Will you come and see me again, Anita?'

As she looked down at the little face smiling up at her, she forgot all the heart-rending problems of her relationship with his father. Kneeling down, eye to eye with the little boy, she told him that, of course, she would come again to see him. Josh put out his arms and gave her a hug.

'You're nice,' he said.

'So are you.'

As she stood up Dan came across to join the huddle by the door. There was an enigmatic expression on his face that Anita couldn't begin to understand. Had she overstepped the mark by agreeing to return? Too late. She'd made a promise to Josh, not to his father, and she never broke a promise made to a child.

Samaya was holding open the front door when she got downstairs.

'Goodnight, Dr Sutherland.'

'Goodnight, Samaya.'

She walked swiftly out to the waiting taxi.

Sleep evaded Anita for a long time after she went to bed. She didn't have a problem with unfamiliar surroundings. She'd always coped well with new situations. It was the intrusion of an old situation upon this new life that was the problem. How to start afresh when the old problems were still there.

She switched on the bedside light and surveyed the chaos of her half-opened suitcase, her clothes from the evening strewn over a chair, the door wide open to her small sitting room showing more clothes in various states of disarray. Tomorrow morning she'd make an effort to create order in this chaos before she went into the hospital.

Before she had to meet up with Dan again. She felt the emotional churning beginning again inside her. How could he do this to her? How could he? When he'd left her because he'd said it was impossible for him to give her the family she wanted. And now she'd found he'd married someone else and had a child. Had he simply made up an excuse to end their relationship?

She got up and went through the sitting room to the small kitchenette where she found a kettle tucked away in a corner. Someone had thoughtfully put some teabags in a jar.

She allowed her thoughts to flutter through her mind as she leaned against the draining board and sipped the hot tea. She recognised that she'd hit rock bottom again in her emotional journey. But she'd been there before and she knew she could drag herself back to normality in the morning. As soon as she slung her stethoscope around her neck, all would be well. Her professional self would take over and she wouldn't allow all this futile emotion to cloud her judgement.

CHAPTER THREE

DAN switched off his office computer and leaned back in his chair. That was enough paperwork for this morning. He planned to delegate the rest to his secretary. He was a doctor and organising schedules and paperwork took up too much valuable time. When he'd first come back to India from America, where he'd had a demanding surgical post, he'd hoped there wouldn't be too much administrative work to keep him from actually treating patients, but it had been a forlorn hope.

He took a sip of the coffee his secretary had placed on his desk some time ago. The air-conditioning had cooled it down to tepid, which made it unpalatable, so it must have been there longer than he'd thought.

He'd come in early so that he could get the boring work out of the way before he started on his clinical rounds. Yes, it had been very early when he'd quietly left the house, long before his now perfectly healthy son had stirred in his sleep. If only he himself could have slept as Josh had last night. The few hours he'd managed had been fraught with dreams from his past life. Bella, his wife who'd died all those years ago, had been in his dreams, telling him he should have told Anita he couldn't have children a lot sooner than he did when she was obviously going to be part of his life.

This was only echoing his own thoughts. He knew now, with the benefit of hindsight, what he should have done. In those first few heady months he shouldn't have waited until they'd been so madly in love with each other that it had been impossible to make rational decisions. It had only been on that fateful evening when Anita, for the first time, had started to talk about how much she longed to have children that he'd known he had to tell her about his vasectomy.

Since falling in love with Anita, he'd seen

several specialists about the possibility of a reversal but the answer at the time had always been negative. So, when Anita had brought up the subject of children, he'd known that he would have to be the strong one who ended the relationship so that she could live her life to the full with someone else. He'd loved her too much to deny her dream of having a family of her own. He'd been heartbroken.

He sighed and took another sip of the dreadful coffee without thinking about it, then pushed it to one side where he couldn't reach it again and poured himself a glass of iced water from the Thermos jug. Everything was quiet around him, just a slight humming sound from the air-conditioning. Distant voices at the end of the corridor were staying out of earshot, thank goodness, and obviously didn't require his attention. He would allow himself the luxury of thinking about the wonderful woman who'd just come back into his life, and what he was going to do about this deep emotional turmoil he found himself in.

When he'd first met Anita he'd been emotionally raw after Bella's death three years previously. She'd come into his life like a breath of fresh air. If you were the sort of person who believed in love at first sight then that was what it must have been. He'd looked down from the podium of the lecture theatre where he'd been teaching a group of medical students and noticed this vibrant young woman who hadn't taken her eyes off him throughout the entire lecture. Every time he'd turned her way he'd seen that she had still been looking at him, sort of gazing at him, which he'd found very flattering because she'd looked absolutely gorgeous. No boyfriend sitting beside her, which had surprised him. A woman like that…

He smiled at the memory of how increasingly difficult he'd found it to concentrate on what he'd been saying. Then, at the end of his lecture, when he'd asked for questions, her hand had shot up and she'd asked him a long complicated one—he couldn't remember what it was now. He'd given her an answer which hadn't seemed to satisfy her because she'd come straight back with another query on the same subject. He'd suggested she stay behind as the questions she'd posed would take some time to answer properly and there had been other students waiting to speak to him.

He remembered he'd suggested coffee when the other students had gone and the session had finally ended. He'd walked with her to the door of the lecture theatre…and that had been when it had all started. He took a deep breath as he remembered how he'd never wanted their relationship to end.

There was someone knocking at his door. It was time to stop daydreaming and become professional again. He frowned as he came back to the present.

'Anita!' He held the door open.

Anita hovered nervously on the threshold. 'You sound surprised. You did ask me to come to your office before I went into A and E.'

'Yes, but it's so early. I wasn't expecting you for at least another half-hour.' He held the door wider. 'Please, do come in. I can't recommend the coffee but…'

'I'm OK, thanks. I've just had breakfast.'

He strode back to his desk, trying to assume a professional attitude which he was finding extremely difficult after allowing himself to dwell on memories of their previous relationship.

'Yes, I felt I hadn't given you much idea of what to expect while you're working here.'

She followed him to sit down at the other side of his desk, watching his long suntanned fingers toying with a pen. He seemed as nervous as she was feeling. She remembered how the ice had melted between them last night in the restaurant. But everything had changed when she'd discovered he had a son. He surely realised how devastated she must be feeling. But they were two professionals here to talk about work and she must give him one hundred per cent of her concentration.

She succeeded in listening to his outline of the work in A and E, occasionally asking a question if there was something she wasn't clear about. But the more he elaborated about the situation at the Rangalore hospital the more confident she became that she could handle whatever came her way. The hospital may have undergone some updating since her father's day but she'd kept pace with such developments in her London hospital. As if reading her thoughts, Dan seemed to echo how she'd summed up her new situation.

'Basically, we'll be calling on all the skills you've learned since you first went into A and E in England, plus the knowledge you have about this part of the world,' Dan was saying as he began to draw his briefing to a close. 'You're at an advantage to most of the English doctors who come out here with very little idea about life in India. That will have been one of the reasons why the medical agency in London chose you.'

She smiled. 'Probably. I mean I don't expect my basic qualifications were any better than those of the other candidates.'

He leaned forward. 'Ah, but you've had a wealth of experience in A and E. I've had time to read the notes that the agency sent since we spoke yesterday. I don't know how you managed to fit everything in during the years since…well, I mean you got married and…and…'

'And then I was widowed,' she put in evenly. 'So I needed to keep working at something I was trained to do, something that would take my mind off the fact that I was alone again.'

He reached across the desk and took hold of her hand. All semblance of professionalism had vanished between them as she raised her eyes to his, knowing she shouldn't have put her hand anywhere near the desk, knowing—or was she hoping?—there was a possibility he might clasp it.

'You had a raw deal when Mark died.'

'It wasn't easy,' she said evenly. 'But I was able to cope. I'd had a hard time when my previous boyfriend dumped me by a letter which instructed me not to try and contact him.'

She cleared her throat, knowing she was now entering dangerous territory. She ought to stop her harangue now before she showed Dan just how much she'd been hurt, and more importantly just how much she still cared. But she couldn't stop now! Not when she'd opened up the old wounds that had festered deep inside her for too long.

She tried to speak dispassionately but failed completely as the awful memories of that bleak period in her life flooded back.

'I'm having a hard time now coming to terms with the fact that this was simply an excuse to get rid of me because how else can you explain the fact that you have a son? How could you go on to—?'

'Excuse me, Dr Mackintosh,' Dan's secretary said as she opened the communicating doors and moved into the room. 'Would you like some fresh coffee?'

Dan ran a hand distractedly through his thick brown hair. 'Yes, yes, Sunita. Coffee for two would be an excellent idea.'

Sunita smiled as she clasped her hands over the silk skirt of her sari. A diminutive figure, she prided herself on her efficiency and Dan found her help invaluable. But at this moment he simply wished she would leave him to sort things out with Anita.

'Very good, sir. It will take me a few minutes to prepare the cafetière.'

Dan forced a smile as he tried to remain polite. He needed someone calm like Sunita to keep the office running like clockwork so he mustn't offend her.

'Take as long as you like, Sunita,' he said.

As soon as the door closed he stood up and went round to the other side of the desk. Placing his hands on Anita's shoulders, he almost lifted her out of her chair until she was standing facing him.

'Dan, I didn't mean to bring up the past…not here at the hospital anyway,' she said, totally confused by the way she'd lost control of her emotions and said far more than she'd intended to. 'It was all a long time ago and I'm trying so hard to forget everything that happened because otherwise we'll never be able to work together. And I do want to stay out here in India. I don't want to admit defeat and have to go back to my old life where…'

She broke off as the reality of the years without Dan hit her once again. Here he was, oh, so close to her. She could feel his hot breath on her face, smell that faint scent of his aftershave. Any moment now she felt she would wake up and find this was all a dream.

His hands were still on her arms. He drew her towards him until he could feel her heart beating against his chest. She was wearing a clean white cotton coat. He could smell her scent. He couldn't help wondering what she was wearing underneath. Probably just bra and briefs because of the heat in the hospital areas which didn't have air-conditioning. His breathing quickened.

He would have to be made of stone not to want her. His desire for her had never faltered over the years and here she was in his arms. He leaned down and cupped her face in his hands as he placed his lips against hers.

Anita continued to feel as if she was dreaming. For a few precious moments she allowed herself to revel in the sensual torture of his lips before she pulled herself away and looked up into his eyes.

'Dan, that won't solve anything,' she said. 'You always thought you could get round me if…if you…'

Sunita was tapping lightly on the door. Dan gave a sigh of exasperation and moved back to his chair.

'Come in!'

The coffee was placed on the table. Precious time elapsed as the secretary poured out the coffee, making sure it was just as they both liked it. As soon as they were alone again, Dan stood up but Anita shook her head.

'Dan, please, stay where you are. As I was saying, it won't solve anything if we try to turn the clock back. You rejected me before—'

'I didn't reject you! I ended our relationship because I couldn't give you the children you wanted so much, and I thought I never would. I loved you too much to deny you that.'

'I remember I'd been more or less living in your flat for about three months,' Anita said. 'You'd told me early on in our relationship that you'd been happily married before but your wife had died three years previously of a congenital cardiac defect. I didn't want to know anything about your marriage. I sensed that it would make you sad to talk about it and anyway I was only interested in our life together, present and future. I brought up the subject of children after about three months because I thought it was time to find out how you felt about it and—'

'And that was when I immediately told you about my vasectomy. I told you that it had been necessary because it would have been too dangerous for my wife to undergo childbirth. I told you that soon after you'd moved in I went to see a specialist to determine if there was any chance of a reversal, but I was told it was impossible.'

'Yes, I remember all that. But let me get this straight. Years after you told me you couldn't father children, we meet up again and I find you have a son and are trying your best to be the perfect father. A child who must have been miraculously conceived after we split up.'

'Anita, I went to America to work but also to search out specialists who might be able to reverse my operation in spite of the complications. I'd exhausted the possibility of a reversal in the UK and the possibility of success in the States was too nebulous for me to worry you with it. I thought it best that I go it alone and if by some miracle I was made fertile then I would find you again.'

He paused. 'But I found out that you were married.'

She swallowed hard. 'And what about the mother of your child? Josh said she was a doctor. Does she work here at the hospital? Will you introduce me as your ex-girlfriend or do you want to keep our previous relationship a secret?'

Dan's desk phone was ringing. He ignored it.

'Hadn't you better answer that?' Anita said, trying to regain some sense of normality. In one way she felt ashamed of her tirade but in another she felt better for having got it off her chest! But she felt exhausted at having expended so much emotional energy and she needed to cool down for a while.

Dan was listening to the voice on the phone. 'Yes, I have Dr Sutherland with me now so it won't be a problem. We'll be with you in a few minutes… Yes, I understand. We'll be as quick as possible.'

Anita was intrigued. She'd barely started work at the hospital so who was wanting to see her? Whoever it was, it was good timing, because she didn't want Dan to make any more revelations at the moment. She wanted to distance herself from this emotionally charged discussion and get back to her work where she'd been trained to keep complete control of her emotions.

As Dan stood up and came round the desk, Anita hurried to her feet and made towards the door. 'I gather we have to go somewhere,' she said.

Dan reached a hand towards her but she evaded him and walked to the door, standing absolutely still as she waited for him to explain.

'That was Sister Banesa from our emergency maternity unit. Jane, the English patient whose baby we delivered yesterday after the RTA, has been asking to see both of us about some problem that's worrying her.'

'Let's go, sir,' Anita said, deliberately assuming a distant, professional voice, with the sort of deference she might use towards her boss.

A brief smile flickered over Dan's face. This

time when he reached out a hand towards her she took it.

'Let's be friends until we can have a proper discussion about the past,' he said, his voice husky with emotion. 'My relationship with Josh's mother wasn't like ours.'

'OK, truce,' she murmured, as he fell into step beside her. As they walked together to the maternity unit they both remained silent, locked in their own thoughts that couldn't possibly be voiced until they were alone again in a non-working environment.

Sister Banesa in emergency maternity directed them to Jane's bed in the corner of a small unit of four beds. Anita decided that the man sitting in a chair beside the bed must be the husband Jane had so desperately been asking for the previous day. He was holding his wife's hand and talking earnestly to her, as if trying to reassure her.

'Oh, Dr Sutherland!' Jane reached out and held onto Anita's hand. 'I'm so glad you came…and you, too, Dr Mackintosh. I was telling Carl, my husband, that I was sure you'd be able to sort something out for me.'

Jane's husband stood up and introduced himself to Anita and Dan before stepping to one side so that they could be nearer their patient.

Anita was alarmed to see the tears beginning to flow down her patient's cheeks. She picked up a tissue from the box on the bedside cabinet and handed it to Jane, who dabbed ineffectively at her damp face.

'So what's the problem, Jane?' Dan said gently.

Jane sniffed. 'I don't want to go home yet because Carl has to go away again on business and I've no idea how to look after my baby. He's in the nursery now, being fed by the nurses because I haven't got the hang of breastfeeding yet. Don't get me wrong. I want to breastfeed but Matthew simply doesn't latch on when I try to plug him in and—'

'Hold on a minute, Jane,' Dan said. 'Nobody's said anything about you going home yet. You had a traumatic day yesterday being involved in a traffic accident and then you had a baby who was two weeks premature. What ever gave you the idea we were going to send you home soon?'

'Well, I was talking to my sister in England on the phone this morning and she said she was only in hospital for six hours after giving birth before she was sent home.'

'Jane, Jane,' Anita said gently. 'Slow down and listen. Nothing like that is going to happen to you. You will be staying in hospital until we assess that you're absolutely fit to go home.'

'But one of the nurses told me this is just an extension of A and E. Patients don't stay here very long.'

'That's correct,' Dan said. 'Patients either go home from here in the emergency unit if they've been treated effectively or they're transferred to a ward appropriate to their medical or surgical problem. We're waiting for a bed for you in the maternity ward.'

Jane gave a sigh of relief. 'You're absolutely sure?'

Dan patted his patient's hand. 'Absolutely

positive. And I'm still in charge of your care until you're admitted to the next ward.'

Jane gave a tentative smile. 'Well, that's OK, then.'

Anita leaned towards her patient. 'Jane, I'll have a word with Sister Banesa. We'll get you some help with breastfeeding. It can seem difficult at first when you feel as if you don't know what's going on,' Anita said. 'With a first baby you think it should come naturally but often it doesn't. You have to work on it.'

'Exactly! I felt guilty that I couldn't stop Matthew from crying. I mean, what sort of a mother am I?'

'You're a new mother who's learning how to cope. Lots of new mothers feel like you do but you'll soon get the hang of things. The first few days are often very bewildering.'

Anita sat down on the edge of the bed and handed Jane another tissue as the tears came again.

Jane smiled up at Anita. 'Have you got children?'

'No.' Anita swallowed hard, very much aware that Dan was standing beside her.

'I'm surprised. You seem to know just exactly how I'm feeling.'

'No, I've been too busy with my work since I qualified as a doctor to find time for children.'

'One day perhaps,' Jane said.

Anita stood up and said she was going to have a word with Sister Banesa.

After a short discussion with the helpful sister of the emergency unit, Anita went back to Jane to reassure her that she was going to get extra help from the nursing staff from now on.

Dan, who'd been dealing with the queries of another patient, on the emergency ward held open the door and followed Anita out.

'I'd like to follow up Jane's case when she moves on to the ward,' Anita told Dan as they walked together down the corridor that led to A and E. 'Is that OK with you, Dan?'

'Absolutely! No reason why you shouldn't if you can fit it in with your work in A and E. But...' He hesitated. 'Don't become too involved...emotionally, I mean.'

He stopped walking and put his hand on her

arm. 'Our involvement with the patients who come in as emergencies carries on while they're in the emergency unit and after that we hand them on to the relevant staff in the wards. We're not expected to—'

'I know we're not expected to do anything else for our patients when we've got them to the wards, but I think sometimes that certain problems raised in the initial time of their stay in hospital should be followed through. For instance, I feel that Jane is feeling so insecure that she could well be a prime candidate for post-natal depression.'

'I certainly hope not,' Dan said firmly as he began striding along the corridor again.

Anita hurried to keep up with him, unable to decide why his manner had changed so abruptly.

'So do I,' she said breathlessly as she caught up again. 'That's why I want to follow up her case. Sometimes telltale clinical signs are missed by the busy staff intent on caring for the physical needs of the patient and her new baby.'

'That's very true,' Dan said, his voice grim. He

hesitated before adding quietly, 'Josh's mother developed postnatal depression.'

'How awful! What did you do about it?'

He pushed through the swing doors leading to A and E before answering her question. 'That again is another long story. We need to get together for a whole evening some time soon so that I can…'

'Answer all my questions?'

He smiled. 'Something like that. Who knows? You might even start to like me again.'

She smiled back but remained silent. Her heart was thumping so loudly he would have heard if there hadn't been so much noise going on in A and E.

'Dr Mackintosh! Dan! Over here, please!'

One of the nursing staff was hanging onto a young man who was trying to evade her grasp. Dan hurried away to help her. Anita could see the patient was drunk. Even though it was early in the day there were certain groups of unemployed youngsters who had taken to drinking cashew fenny, which was easily available and very cheap.

Anita went across to the nursing station. Sister Razia immediately asked her to attend to a patient who'd been waiting to see a doctor.

Anita examined the man as he lay on the couch. The man spoke quietly in English. He told Anita his name was Abdul. He was fifty-five and lived in a small village near Rangalore. He'd been teaching in the village school all his adult life.

'They found somebody younger than me to do my job,' Abdul told her. 'I've got a small pension—just enough to live on because my wife has died and I live on my own. I don't need much. My children include me in their family life when they can. But they were all too busy to come with me today. So I took the bus into town.'

He stopped speaking and grimaced as a spasm of pain ran through him.

'Tell me where you hurt.'

'I've been feeling bad for a couple of days. Keep getting this pain in my back. I saw the doctor in my village but he didn't know what it was so I came here. The doctor told me to rest but when I rest I worry. Better to keep moving. What do you think, Doctor?'

Anita said she would have to examine him before she could give an opinion. She examined his spine thoroughly but couldn't find any lesions. She was just about to arrange an X-ray of his spine when Dan came into the cubicle. She took advantage of the fact that a second opinion was always a good idea.

Dan listened to her description of the symptoms before suggesting that she should also include a chest X-ray.

'A chest X-ray? But his pain is in his back.'

He drew her to one side. 'I once had a patient who had been complaining of back pain which had come on suddenly. I couldn't find anything wrong with his back—like our patient here. So I assumed it might be referred pain from the chest—or even the heart.'

'And were you right?'

Dan nodded. 'There was a lesion in the aorta which showed up on the X-ray. I operated the same day and as far as I know he's still alive.'

'But what makes you think this case might be similar?'

Dan frowned. 'You can never be sure till you've done all the tests, can you? By which time it could be too late. The signs and symptoms of this case are very nebulous but it would be a mistake not to treat the possibilities I've outlined. Let's rule out the involvement of other parts of the body before we assume this is a simple case of back strain.'

Their patient across the other side of the cubicle called out for a drink of water. Dan went back to speak to Abdul. 'We'd better have you X-rayed before you start drinking. If you need an operation you'll need an empty stomach. I'll come back to see you when you've come back from X-Ray.'

Anita took care of another patient while Abdul was away. Her new patient, an English woman in her fifties, had arrived on holiday the previous evening and while lifting in her luggage from the coach to the hotel had stepped into a drainage ditch that was obscured by plants in a dimly lit section of the hotel garden.

From the unnatural angle of the ankle it was easy to diagnose a fracture of one or more of the bones. Anita asked one of the nurses to accompany the porter and the patient to X-Ray.

Abdul had just returned with his X-rays and was back in his cubicle. Anita paged Dan, who arrived shortly afterwards as she was taking some blood from her patient for testing. He picked up the X-rays and displayed them on the screen.

Standing back to get the best view, he pointed to the one that displayed the aorta to best advantage.

'Look here, Anita!' He was pointing at one section of the aorta closest to the heart. He lowered his voice. 'We've got no time to lose. I'll alert the cardiac team to get a theatre ready as soon as possible.'

'It looks like an aneurism,' Anita said quietly as Dan drew her to one side. 'In which case…'

'Exactly! It could rupture at any time, which is why we need to get Abdul to Theatre. I'll get the theatre and the team, you explain to the patient.'

Dan had got through to the cardiac team 'Yes, Sister, it's Dan here, and I need that theatre now!'

In the next few minutes they arranged everything and Abdul was taken to Theatre with essential pre-op preparation only.

Anita went back to her patient with the fractured ankle. The X-rays showed that the calcaneum, the heel bone, had shattered on impact with the bottom of the drainage ditch. Some of the fragments of bone had protruded into the space between the calcaneum and the smaller bone above it. This meant that there would be some problem with the joint when eventually the patient was able to walk again. But for the moment the main problem was getting a cast on the ankle to hold it in place.

Again she called on Dan for a second opinion. 'Do you think we need to put a couple of pins in this heel to prevent the bone fragments from moving up into the intra-articular space any more than they have done?'

Dan nodded. 'Well, that's what I would do. If we can hold the depressed articular fragments of the calcaneum in place, there shouldn't be any loss of height.'

'That could be done under an epidural an-aesthetic, couldn't it?'

Dan nodded. 'It certainly could. I'll get through to the orthopaedic firm and see how they're fixed today. I'll report back to you on that one.'

He paused at the door of the cubicle as he went out. 'Will you be free this evening for our clinical discussion?'

He said it so gravely she was almost taken in. 'What…? Oh, that!'

'Yes, that!'

'I've got to get sorted out so…I don't think I'll have time tonight because…'

'It's got to be tonight because I need to give you all the facts. You keep looking at me as if I… Look, you've got to eat at some point tonight. Come home with me and have some supper. Oh, it's OK. We won't be alone! I've told Samaya I'll be late tonight so she's going to put Josh to bed and prepare supper for me. I'll let her know you'll be with me.'

'Mmm, the thought of being pampered with a prepared supper at the end of a long day is very tempting,' she said carefully. 'I suppose I could continue to live in my chaotic room for a bit longer before I can find the time to sort it out.'

'Of course you could!'

CHAPTER FOUR

ANITA breathed a sigh of relief as she eased herself into the passenger seat in Dan's car.

'That was a day and a half!'

Dan smiled as he let in the clutch. 'You should be used to that sort of non-stop day by now.'

'Oh, don't get me wrong. I am used to the continual pressure of A and E. It's just that, well, it didn't seem as if we were ever going to get away.'

She stopped, realising that she'd been about to say how much this evening—or rather what was left of it—had become so significant in the moments when she'd been able to give a thought to her own personal situation.

Fortunately, Dan was concentrating on trying to squeeze the car through a tiny space where an ambulance was awkwardly parked near the front gate of the hospital.

'Sorry, what were you saying?' he asked as he gathered speed on the main road.

'Oh, I've forgotten now,' she said hurriedly. 'Did you manage to organise an operation for Catherine with the fractured calcaneum? I saw you taking her away at one point but I was too busy to follow up her case.'

'I liaised with the orthopaedic firm and we decided to operate tomorrow. There are a number of tests we need to do first before we fix the ankle with the pins. I've put her in a temporary splint until I take her to Theatre. Because of the staffing situation, I've agreed to do the operation early tomorrow when there will be a free theatre.'

'You're going to operate then?'

'Don't sound so surprised! I'm Director of Surgery as well as A and E. That's my job specification. If there's a staffing problem, I fill in where necessary. Actually, I really enjoy getting back into Theatre whenever I can. I'll take any excuse to scrub up and be at the centre of where it's all happening.'

'Yes, I remember your enthusiasm when you gave that first lecture. I don't want to sound as if I'm being sycophantic but we young, wet-behind-the-ears students found you really inspiring. Now, don't get bigheaded, Dan,' she finished off laughingly, 'Perhaps that was a bit over the top but quite a few of my friends decided to go into surgery after listening to you.'

'Well, that's good to know,' he said lightly, as he took a turning off the main road and reduced his speed to deal with the narrow road where his headlights had picked out a cow several metres ahead, ambling slowly out from the grass verge. He brought the car to a halt to allow the animal time to get safely across.

He turned to look at Anita, thinking that she was still as beautiful as she had been on that day—more so, if he was truthful with himself. He loved the way she let her dark brown hair fall on to her shoulders when she was off duty. In hospital she kept it safely tied up in a chignon.

Anyway, there were a couple of faint wrinkles on her forehead, which showed endearingly, he'd noticed, when she worked on something that required deep concentration in hospital—suturing a wound or even writing a short report on a patient. But this newfound maturity made her even more desirable to him. He knew she'd suffered over the years and he wanted so much to make it up to her—if she would let him!

He leaned across so that he could put one hand on the back of her seat. 'I have to say, that on that particular occasion, all those years ago,' he said, carefully, 'one of my priorities was to make sure I could persuade the intense young student who'd given me all her attention to come out for coffee with me afterwards.'

'And the rest is history,' she said, trying to keep the emotion out of her voice as she became intensely aware of his closeness to her. It was becoming impossible to deal with the sensual stirrings deep down inside her. Dan had always had this effect on her. But she hadn't planned for this to happen. Tonight was about getting some answers to her questions.

She moved in her seat and pointed straight ahead. 'I think that cow has reached safety now and there's a car waiting for us to move on.'

'So there is.' He restarted the engine.

'Anyway, back to the present,' Anita said, as they drove down the narrow road once more. 'So, you're going to operate on Catherine early tomorrow, which is OK because I shan't be staying late. Is she in the emergency unit tonight?'

'No, I got her a room on the orthopaedic ward. We'll need to keep her in for a few days after the operation because it's a complicated case. As you know, the main problem is that the X-rays show that some of the fragments from the calcaneum have intruded into the intra-articular space. I'll have to try and hold the bone fragments back when I insert the pins. And because Catherine has osteoporosis, we'll have to leave the pins in longer than usual.'

'But fortunately Catherine's general health seems OK, apart from the very obvious signs of osteoporosis on the X-rays that I saw.'

'Yes, as I just said, that's going to delay the healing of the bones but she's having extra medication for the osteoporosis.' Dan took one hand off the wheel and placed it on her arm. 'Just relax now and stop thinking about work. You've done enough for one day.'

'Just one final question about work and then I'll switch off. Don't you feel pleased that you checked out Abdul so thoroughly when he'd simply came in complaining of back pain?'

'Ah, well, that was my own past experience that helped me. If I hadn't come up against the same symptoms before, I may not have hypothesised about a possible cardiac aneurism. Years ago, I remember a doctor in England actually sent one of his patients home with painkillers for her back pain and recommended she see an osteopath. Fortunately, her husband was also a doctor and had formed his own diagnosis. So we didn't lose the patient—on that occasion. It taught me never to assume the obvious when you're making a diagnosis.'

She frowned as she noted the intensity of his tone. 'Was this doctor anybody I might know?'

'I'll tell you all about it later,' he said evenly, as he reached for the gear lever to change down.

They were driving through the gates of Dan's house and up the winding drive with its palm trees set back along the sides to give shelter from the sun. Anita pressed the automatic button on the passenger door to open the window. She wanted to change the cool, unnatural atmosphere of the air-conditioning for the real Indian evening temperature.

She breathed in the cooling air, scented with a faint hint of the frangipani that grew in front of the magnificent building.

'It's a beautiful house!'

'Yes, I was lucky to find it soon after we moved here from Mumbai.'

'Who's we?'

'Josh and Samaya and me.'

'So Samaya was with you in Mumbai?'

'Of course. I was lucky that she agreed to come with us. She actually moved her retired parents down here at the same time. They took a small house in Rangalore. She's been with us since we moved to India from America. Continuity of care for Josh is very important, don't you think?'

'Absolutely!' She hesitated. 'So Josh's mother is still in America?'

'Yes, she is.' Dan switched off the engine, remembering the letter he'd had a couple of days ago. 'We divorced while Joshua was still a baby. So I haven't seen her for a long time.'

As he stepped out of the car he was wondering if all that was about to change. Rachel's timing couldn't have been worse but he would cope with that when he had to. For the moment he owed it to Anita to put her in the picture and worry about the impending visit when it happened.

Samaya opened the door, her calm face lighting up with a smile as they walked from the car to the house.

'Welcome,' she said softly. 'Supper is ready, Dan. Would you like me to serve it now? It's just soup, followed by salad and cold chicken. I thought it best to keep things simple as you weren't sure when you would be here.'

'Thank you, Samaya. I'll serve supper myself

after we've had a drink on the veranda. Why don't you take yourself off and relax now? Is Josh asleep?'

'I think he's trying to stay awake until you come.'

Dan smiled. 'I'll go up to see him.'

'He also said he wanted to see the pretty lady that Daddy brought home.' Samaya was walking towards the doorway. She turned with an apologetic expression on her face. 'I'm afraid I let slip the fact that you were bringing someone home tonight.'

'That's OK, Samaya. I think he means you, Anita. It's a long time since I brought a pretty lady home.'

Anita followed Dan up the ornate staircase and along the wide landing. They stopped outside the little boy's room. Dan peeped round the door to check whether his son was still awake.

'Hi, little man! I thought you might be asleep.' Dan strode inside. 'I've brought Anita to see you.'

Josh sat up in bed, immediately wide awake as Anita crossed to the bed.

'Anita!' The little boy spread his arms wide.

Anita sat down on the bed and found herself enveloped in his embrace. 'What a lovely welcome!'

'I've been trying so hard not to sleep so I could see you.'

'Don't I get a hug tonight?'

'Daddy!'

The resultant huddle of hugs was emotionally warming. Anita felt a current of pure happiness tinged with sadness. This was how it could have been if they'd stayed together. She could have given Dan a son like Josh. But the way she was feeling towards this little boy was almost maternal already. He was finding his way into her heart and there was nothing she could do about that.

She gently disentangled herself from the boy's arms and stood up.

'Please, don't go, Anita,' Josh said. 'Please, will you read me a story?'

She smiled down at him. 'Of course. What stories have you got up here?'

Dan was looking through the books in Josh's bedside cabinet. 'This is a good one and it's not too long. Anita hasn't had any supper yet so she must come down soon.'

'OK, OK,' Josh said excitedly, thumbing through the story till he came to the picture he was looking for. 'It's all about this tiger. Start here, Anita, this is the best bit. Don't be scared— it's a nice tiger really. You'll like him when you read about him.'

Anita found herself sitting on the bed again, one arm around Josh and the other hand holding the book. Josh followed the story, with her turning the pages when necessary. Once, when she turned two pages at once, he corrected her.

Dan smiled. 'You can't skip a page when you're reading to Josh. I'll say goodnight now.'

He bent down and kissed his son on the top of his head, his hand lightly brushing Anita's arm as he moved away.

'Daddy, are you bringing Anita to the beach with us on Sunday?'

'That will depend on whether Anita is free,' Dan said carefully. 'I do know she's not on duty that day but she may have made other plans.'

'Anita, have you got other plans?' Josh asked excitedly. 'Please, say you haven't because I know you'll like the beach!'

Dan was standing by the door, looking across at her. 'We'd really like you to come with us.'

Her eyes locked with his. 'As far as I know, I think I can make it.'

'Good! Daddy you'll tell Anita what to bring, won't you? You know, swimsuits and buckets and spades and footballs and stuff like that.'

'I'll see to it, Josh. Now, you go back to your story and then you must go straight to sleep.'

Anita continued reading as she heard Dan going downstairs. Towards the end of the story she sensed that Josh was falling asleep. Looking up from the page, she saw his eyes were closing. When she leaned over to give him a goodnight kiss he opened his eyes briefly and murmured something incoherent before sinking back against the pillow, fast asleep.

As she tiptoed out of the bedroom, the feeling of sadness returned. This was all she could ever hope for with Dan. Whatever revelations he made tonight wouldn't explain away the fact that he'd ended their relationship before and he might do so again. But this was why she'd come here tonight, to get the truth. For no other reason.

As she went down the stairs she admitted to herself that this wasn't really true. She was once more besotted with the infuriating man!

She found him on the veranda that stretched the length of the back of the house.

'Good timing!'

He reached for the bottle of wine from the ice bucket at the side of the wicker table and began to uncork it.

'Come and sit over here, Anita.'

She sank down into one of the comfy wicker chairs, the cushions enveloping her so that she began to relax. He handed her a glass of wine and she took a sip, then another one as the unwinding process continued.

'Mmm! I feel really off duty now. My, you have been busy!'

She surveyed the supper he'd set out on the table. Cold chicken, a large bowl of salad, chapattis, samosas, various pickles set out in small dishes and soup bowls set before the two places.

'Not really! I only had to carry it here from the kitchen. I'll go and get the soup.'

He returned and stood beside her chair ready to serve her. 'It's vegetable soup highly seasoned with a variety of strong spices—one of Samaya's secret recipes, I believe, handed down from mother to daughter.'

She sensed Dan was nervous as he ladled out the soup from a large earthenware tureen before sitting down at the other side of the table.

'Delicious soup!' She looked across at him, thinking how handsome he looked in the candlelight. He'd changed into jeans and a cotton polo shirt and although he looked relaxed she knew him well enough to sense that he was worried about how she was going to take his explanations.

She put down her spoon and picked up her wineglass. 'Shall we talk about why you finished our affair? It might help to clear the air.'

He leaned forward. 'Let's finish supper first.'

'No good putting it off.'

'I'm not trying to procrastinate but I really think you should put something on your plate. Neither of us has eaten during the day and we need our strength. Help yourself, Anita.'

They stuck to light conversational subjects as they ate, deliberately avoiding the main issues. At one point Dan had to leave the table to find a mosquito repellant.

'It must have got in through the mosquito screen when I opened it briefly while you were still with Josh.'

Dan was now climbing up onto a stool, can in hand, taking aim and… 'Gotcha!'

He went across to the washbasin at the side of the veranda and washed his hands before returning to the table.

'One less in the fight against malaria!'

'Absolutely!' She sat very quietly watching

him. 'You've got your serious expression on now so shall we start?'

He raised his hands. 'The question, is where shall I start?'

'Why not go back to the beginning? Once upon a time…'

'Once upon a time there was a man called Dan who was very much in love with—'

'Stick to the point, Dan. Leave out the embroidered bits.'

He picked up a piece of chapatti from his plate and began to pull it apart. 'OK, I'll go right back to the beginning, long before you came on the scene.'

She waited. He looked across at her and his gaze was steady as he began to speak again.

'I was married very young to a wonderful girl called Bella. We were both medical students. We were deeply in love. Six months into the marriage she went to the resident medical officer complaining of backache. He recommended she see an osteopath and take painkillers. I didn't even know she'd gone to see him. I remember we were both on different courses at the time and she hadn't discussed it with me.'

'Was this the case we were discussing earlier?'

He nodded. 'When she came back to the flat that night and told me, I was immediately alerted to the facts she'd told me earlier in our marriage.'

Anita leaned forward. 'Which were?'

'One time when she was playing hockey at school she'd fainted. The school doctor sent her to hospital for tests. It transpired that she'd had an aortic aneurism since birth. After numerous tests it was decided that it would be too dangerous to operate and so she must avoid strenuous exercise for the rest of her life. Bella hadn't made the connection between the back pain and her delicate health.'

'And neither, apparently, had the resident medical officer you were telling me about.'

'Exactly! I asked Bella if she'd explained her previous medical history when she'd seen the doctor that morning. She said she hadn't thought it relevant and she'd wanted to get back for a lecture. I pointed out that it could be referred pain from her aortic aneurism. In the end I insisted she be admitted to our hospital for a full examination.'

He paused and took a deep breath. 'The diagnosis was confirmed. The pain was coming from an inoperable aortic aneurism. She was advised to discontinue her medical studies and take life easy. She was also told that having children wasn't an option. It would be life-threatening for her.'

Again he paused and gripped the table. As Anita watched him, struggling to find the right words, she saw the glistening of his tears in the candlelight.

'That was when I had the vasectomy.'

They were both silent. Seconds elapsed. There wasn't a sound. An ice cube shifted in the bucket and crunched down onto the ice below. Somewhere out in the garden an owl hooted. The ceiling fan whirred softly above them.

She looked down at the table. His gaze was raw with sadness.

'I wish you'd told me more of this when we...when we first started...seeing each other.'

'Anita, I couldn't tell you. I was still grieving for Bella when I met you. And I didn't know we were going to become, well, practically inseparable. Neither did I know how deeply you felt about having children until that evening when…'

'When you told me you'd had a vasectomy and we started to discuss how we were going to deal with being a childless couple and—'

'And I took you home, not having resolved anything but knowing we had to take some time out to think about a solution or whether we should part.'

'And you resolved the situation by calling an immediate halt in the form of a letter, setting out the parameters. You were going to America and I wasn't to try to contact you.'

'Anita, that was the hardest thing I've ever had to do. But I thought only of your happiness. I wanted you to have the freedom to find someone else who could fulfil your dreams of having a family.'

She remained silent, willing herself to believe him. But her trust had been broken all those years ago and she was still raw with negative emotion. Seconds elapsed before she was able to speak.

'So, how did you manage to father a child?'

He took a deep breath. 'I visited several more specialists in America until I found one who said he would give it a try but didn't hold out much hope.'

'And he was successful?'

Dan nodded. 'Yes, but it was too late. I'd heard you were about to get married.'

'When you went to America, I saw no possibility of us getting back together again ever. You'd made that perfectly clear. Initially, Mark had simply been there to pick up the pieces for me, a shoulder to cry on. We both knew I didn't love him in the way I'd loved you. But he had so much love to give. He told me he had love enough for both of us. He was a great comfort to me. I wanted to make him a good wife and have a happy life together.'

As she dabbed at her eyes with her napkin, Dan stood up and hurried round the table, gently drawing her to her feet, cradling her in his arms.

'I'm sorry, I don't know how to convince you how it was but…'

'Oh, I can see why you acted as you did, why you couldn't see any future for us.'

He had drawn her towards a comfortable sofa near the table, settling her beside him still with one arm cradled around her. She felt the warmth and excitement of his body and knew it would make sense to move away. But she was incapable of destroying the wonderful rapport that was developing between them.

'Had the specialist already told you that the reversal of vasectomy operation had been a complete success by this time?'

'Yes.' He was breathing deeply. 'He told me I had a healthy sperm count again and that as far as he knew there was now no reason why I couldn't become a father. He suggested I tell my partner the good news and try for a baby.'

She frowned. 'What partner?'

'Exactly! I didn't tell him that I'd just heard the woman I loved was going to be married in a few days and I had definitely not been invited to the wedding. I even thought of turning up and disrupting the service, like they do in films and TV soaps, storming up to the altar and sweeping you off your feet, carrying you away in my arms and lifting you up onto my white horse…'

She couldn't help smiling. 'I'm not sure…'

'But I assumed you were both madly in love and I didn't have the right to disrupt anything. Mark was a good man?'

'Yes, he was,' she said quietly. 'One of the best.'

They remained silent for a while, very aware of the closeness of each other. Anita's emotions were in turmoil again as she tried to come to terms with Dan's revelations.

'So tell me about how you met Josh's mother. What's her name?'

'Rachel. We were colleagues at the university hospital in Boston. She was something of an academic blue stocking, had studied continually since she was in her cradle, I think. She comes from a good family. Her father was dean of the university, her mother was a professor of bio-chemistry—all that kind of thing.'

Anita smiled. 'You sound as if you had reservations about Rachel and her family.'

'That's putting it mildly. I was completely overawed by them.'

'But there must have been some romance to have got you as far as getting married.'

'At first it was purely platonic,' he said carefully. 'We were colleagues who enjoyed going out for a meal together, seeing a show, going to a concert—that sort of thing. Then we became fond of each other—and, yes, it did become romantic after a while.'

Anita tried to come to terms with this, tried to banish the jealous feelings she was experiencing when thinking of another woman in Dan's arms.

'So you decided to get married,' she said quietly.

'Yes, eventually we did. We thought we could make a go of it. Rachel was in her thirties and she pointed out that her biological clock was ticking away all the time and she'd like to have a child. I said so would I. And in the space of a few months we were married and Josh was on the way.'

'And were you happy?'

'At first—but it wasn't like the happiness we'd known when you moved into my flat in London.'

He reached for her and, against all her better judgement, she went willingly into his arms.

A sigh escaped her lips as she felt herself, oh, so deliciously cradled against his chest. She felt powerless to resist him. His arms were so strong as he held her. She knew she only had to move and he would let her go. But she didn't want him to release her. She wanted to stay here, enclosed in this cocoon of love…yes, it was love again. The love she'd carried with her all these years. Sometimes dreaming in her sleep that this longed-for experience would happen again…

He drew her back onto the sofa, his hands gently caressing her as his kisses became more passionate. She knew where this was going and she somehow found the strength to extricate herself from the cushions.

'Dan, we can't turn the clock back.'

He sat up. 'I'm not suggesting we do that.'

'I need to know more about this relationship you have with Rachel.'

'Had with Rachel. After Josh was born she suffered from postnatal depression and couldn't bear to have anything to do with him—or me. I doted on Josh but it was difficult, taking care of him and continuing to work. I had to hire a full-time nurse to look after him during the times I wasn't there.'

'And Rachel?'

'Rachel went back to live with her parents. After a while she decided she was going to go back to work. She'd been offered a good career move in another hospital. Continuing to climb the career ladder would save her sanity, she said. Looking back, I don't think we really examined our feelings enough before we got married and ended up doing so for all the wrong reasons. We agreed that the marriage was over and she was happy for me to have custody of Josh. I haven't had a word from Rachel or her family since Josh was about one. Rachel's mother wrote to say that Rachel had resumed her career and was being very successful.'

'And you've heard nothing since then?'

'Well, strangely enough…'

He paused as he wondered if this was the right time to broach the subject.

'Strangely enough, I got a letter earlier this week from Rachel, saying that she is now professor of surgery at the university. Apparently she often gets invitations to give lectures to students at overseas universities.' He swallowed hard. 'One of the requests this year came from Rangalore University and she has agreed to do it.'

'No!' Anita drew in her breath.

'She also said that she'd like to meet Josh… well, she is his mother, Anita.'

'Of course,' she said blandly. 'When is she coming?'

'In about a month. The dates haven't been set yet.'

'So I shall get to meet your ex-wife.' Anita stood up. 'Look, I'd better be getting back. And you've got an early operation to perform. What time do you start?'

'I've booked the theatre for seven o'clock. I've got an anaesthetist who has already checked out Catherine as suitable for spinal anaesthesia. I've got a good theatre sister and her team but I wondered…'

He had a wry expression on his face as he turned towards her. 'I wondered if you would assist me in the morning. I spoke briefly to one of the doctors who's on night duty at the moment and he agreed to be on standby if I needed him. I wanted to ask you earlier but I didn't know if we'd still be speaking to each other after this evening.'

'I'd like to assist at Catherine's operation so of course I'll do it,' she said evenly. But seven in the morning… She glanced at her watch. 'It's already after midnight. I'd better call a taxi.'

'I've got a proposition to make.'

'No, Dan, I—'

'Stay in the guest room. I promise you can lock the door if you wish. I'll take you to the hospital in the morning. OK?'

She smiled. 'OK.'

He reached out and took her hand, leading her through into the house and walking upstairs.

'Goodnight, Anita,' he said firmly, as he stood

outside one of the bedroom doors. 'There's a bathroom en suite so you won't have to come out on the landing and risk bumping into me. And the key's in the door on the other side.'

He relaxed again as he stooped to kiss her on the lips. 'Goodnight, Anita. I'll call you on your bedside phone in the morning.'

She watched him for a few seconds as he strode away from her down the landing. She could tell he was already in surgeon mode and she knew she had to get some sleep. She sighed heavily as she turned the doorknob and went into the palatial guest suite. It seemed so unnatural for Dan to be heading the other way when they could have been together for the whole night. If only she could get rid of all her reservations about a future with Dan. But she couldn't.

She closed the door softly, removed her shoes and padded across the rich carpet towards the bathroom.

CHAPTER FIVE

'OK, EVERYBODY, thank you all for coming in so early this morning.' Dan looked around the operating theatre at the assembled team. 'How's our patient, Anita?'

Anita looked up from the other end of the operating table where she had been helping the anaesthetist perform the spinal anaesthesia that would remove the sensation from their patient's lower body.

'Catherine's lower body now registers no sensation at all so you can proceed, Dan,' she assured him.

Anita bent over her patient and quietly explained what was happening. 'You can watch what's happening on the screen up there, if you'd like to. I know you told me you used to be a nurse so...'

'Oh, yes!' Catherine turned her head to look up at the screen at the side of the operating table on which she was lying. 'It's strange, having no sensation. When the spinal anaesthetic first started to take effect, my lower body felt a warm rush of sensation—rather like cuddling a hot-water bottle—and then everything went cold. Now there's no sensation at all so it's just like watching someone else have an operation.'

'That's good. I'm going to help Dan to insert the pins now.'

Anita signalled to a nurse to come and stay close to their patient in case she became anxious at any part of the operation. She told the nurse that she didn't expect this would happen but it was routine procedure with this type of operation where the patient was awake.

As she moved further down the operating table she thought how Catherine was the ideal patient. Most patients didn't want to watch the screen to see what was happening and usually closed their eyes until it was all over. They were the ones who needed to hold onto a sympathetic nurse's hand. But Catherine's eyes were glued to the sight of her own foot, which she could now see on the screen.

Dan looked across the table at Anita. 'Everything OK?'

Anita nodded. 'Couldn't be better.'

They had both been in professional mode since meeting earlier in the kitchen of Dan's house for a quick coffee and a bowl of muesli each. They'd continued in virtual silence as they'd driven into the hospital. It was as if the emotional turmoil of the previous evening had never happened. And Anita knew that this was the only way to deal with it. She mustn't allow any distracting thoughts about their personal situation to intrude when they were working together.

With Dan directing her, she turned the back of the patient's heel towards Dan so that he could make the two incisions to accommodate the pins that would prevent the fragments of the fractured calcaneum invading the joint any further.

'Because Catherine's bones are osteoporotic, the pins go in without much resistance,' Dan said as he began inserting them. 'I'm planning to increase her medication to try to strengthen the bones. Because of the osteoporosis, the healing process will take longer but the bones will eventually heal.'

He was watching the screen as he worked, which enabled him to see how far the pins had penetrated the calcaneum. It was a delicate operation but one in which Dan was skilled and experienced, and Anita knew he wouldn't make any mistakes as she handed him the surgical instruments he required.

At the end of the operation Anita stemmed the flow of blood, initially holding a sterile pad over the heel before covering it with a sterile dressing.

'Would you like me to put the temporary immobilising cast on, Dan?'

'Yes, please. I'm holding the foot at exactly the right angle now so you can fix it underneath... Yes, that's great... Now close it over the top.'

'We're fixing a temporary cast over your foot and lower leg, Catherine,' Dan told their patient. 'I'll put a more permanent cast on in about three

days when the swelling has diminished. We'd
like you to stay in the orthopaedic ward where
we can keep an eye on you and make sure you
get the right medication. Is that OK with you?'

'Fine!' Catherine raised herself up on her
elbows. 'I didn't feel a thing. Still can't!'

'Perfect!' Anita said, as she started clearing
away some of the instruments.

Dan leaned across the table. 'I'll see you in A
and E after you've settled Catherine back in the
ward. I want to call in at the cardiac unit to see
how Abdul is recovering from the surgery he
had yesterday.'

Anita nodded. Only then did she allow herself
to relax as she looked at Dan. They'd success-
fully worked together even after the emotional
discussion of the night before. So perhaps she
needn't have worried so much during the night.
During that long night alone in Dan's guest suite,
knowing that he had only been a short distance
along the landing from her, knowing that if she'd
let down her guard and allowed him to…

'Are you all right, Anita?'

'Yes, I'm fine!' She looked across the table at Dan, whose anxious expression was very touching. He really cared about her!

'You looked as if you were going to faint or something.'

'Faint? Not me! I'm as tough as old boots.'

'I don't think old boots describes you at all,' he said softly. 'More like…' Then, as if suddenly remembering where he was, he moved away from the table. 'OK, I'm out of here. Thanks for your help, everybody.'

Anita accompanied her patient back to the ward and stayed to check on her blood pressure and other vital signs.

'I still can't feel my lower body, Anita,' Catherine said, as Anita finished writing up the case notes at the side of her patient's bed. 'Is that normal?'

'It will take a while, Catherine. I'll come back in a couple of hours when the spinal anaesthesia will probably have worn off. That's when you'll need some painkillers.'

Catherine pulled a wry face. 'It would be great

if I could stay like this for a few weeks until all the pain goes away.'

Anita smiled. 'Don't worry, we won't let you suffer.'

On the way back to A and E Anita called into the obstetrics ward to see how Jane was getting on. Her patient was sitting out of bed in an armchair, trying to feed baby Matthew who was definitely being uncooperative.

'Oh, Doctor, I'm glad you've come. I was just about to give up again. I don't think this breast-feeding is going to work. Perhaps I should just let the nurses bottlefeed him.'

'Well, let's give it another try, Jane,' Anita said soothingly, lifting baby Matthew into her arms. 'Are you comfortable in this chair?'

'Not entirely.'

'You need to be comfortable and relaxed. Now, why don't you get yourself comfortable in the bed again? Yes, that's right.'

Anita gently patted the baby's back as she watched his mother climb back into bed and lean back on the pillows. The baby obliged by letting out a resounding burp of wind. That would help him to co-operate with his mother, hopefully!

'Now, Matthew's nice and calm again, so I'll give him back to you and we'll make sure he latches onto your nipple... Yes, be gentle but firm with him... There, he's got the right idea now and he seems hungry.'

'He's feeding, Doctor! I can feel him pulling on my nipple!'

'That's good, very good. You're a natural mother, Jane.'

Anita stayed for a few minutes to reassure her. Calling over one of the nurses, she asked her to stay on to make sure Jane had all the support she needed. She called at the nurses' station on her way out to speak to Sister Banesa and make sure that the message got through that Jane was an extremely anxious patient who could very easily develop a phobia about her baby and possibly go into a state of postnatal depression. Sister agreed that she would alert all her nurses so that they would be sympathetic to Jane's needs.

* * *

Back in A and E Anita was caught up in the aftermath of another road traffic accident, patients being wheeled in on trolleys, wounds to be dealt with in the treatment areas, patients to be soothed before being despatched to Theatre. The patients were from a school bus and the noise of the small patients and their relatives had reached an unprecedented high.

Anita managed to piece together what had happened out there on a bumpy road from one of the outlying villages. A motorbike had overtaken the bus and then cut in front of it too quickly. The driver had swerved to avoid the bike and the bus had gone into a ditch. Fortunately, even though the children had not been wearing seat belts, there had been no fatalities.

By the end of the day Anita was feeling exhausted. She had lost count of how many patients she had treated. But the level of noise was diminishing as patients were admitted to wards or allowed to go home.

'The bone in Fahid's arm will heal well,' she

told one anxious mother, speaking in the Hindi she'd learned as a child.

She was relieved to find the language came back to her very naturally as she pointed out on the X-ray screen where there was a faint crack in the larger of the two bones in the lower arm. Her father had spoken fluent Hindi to his patients and he'd helped Anita learn basic anatomy and physiology from an early age.

'This bone is called the ulna. That little crack will be healed in four to five weeks and then the cast will come off and your son will be good as new.'

As she took her first break of the day, leaning back against the hard wooden chair in one of the cubicles, Dan came in and perched on the edge of the examination couch.

'I've just handed over to the night staff. Are you ready to go off duty?'

'More than ready!'

'I'm going to hurry back to spend some time with Josh. Would you like to come with me?'

'Not tonight Dan. Give my love to Josh and tell

him I'm looking forward to going to the beach with him on Sunday.'

She stood up decisively. If she didn't leave Dan now, she would have second thoughts and find herself back at Dan's house. She needed some time to sort out her thoughts. She was becoming too close, too emotionally involved.

Dan stood up and walked to the door with her, his hand resting lightly in the small of her back.

'Are you sure I can't persuade you to change your mind?'

She smiled up at him. 'Positive. Goodnight, Dan.'

On Sunday morning she woke up as the sun streamed in through the gap in the curtains. She'd fallen asleep the previous night worrying about what she should wear to the beach but now she couldn't think why she'd got so worked up. It was only a trip to the beach with Dan and Josh. She would put on a bikini under her three-quarter-length lightweight jeans teamed with a cotton top and simply enjoy herself.

She remembered the times she'd been to the beach with her parents when she'd been young. The most important thing was that everyone should be relaxed. Just go with the flow and be a child again.

As she climbed out of bed and crossed over to her bathroom, she glanced around her, pleased to see that at last she was getting some sort of order into her domain. The off-duty time she'd devoted to getting organised had paid off. She now had all her clothes in the chest of drawers or the wardrobe and she'd even brought in a bunch of flowers, which were in a large plastic container until she could find something better.

One of the patients had been going home and had insisted Anita take the flowers which had just arrived for her. So there they were in pride of place, pink carnations with green feathery ferns added to set off their colour. She'd salvaged the plastic container from a waste bin, washed it out thoroughly and arranged the bouquet so that the ferny bits hung over the sides. It would do until she had time to go for a vase at the shopping mall in downtown Rangalore.

As she showered in the tiny basic bathroom she couldn't help remembering the palatial bathroom at Dan's house. Wow! Now, that had been something else! Pity she hadn't had time to luxuriate in that enormous bath. If the occasion arose again…

She wrapped a towel round herself as she emerged from the shower. She couldn't help hoping the occasion would arise again but she still had no idea how she intended to deal with it. And it would be even more complex if she found herself in the master bedroom suite. At that point she decided she had to stop daydreaming and be realistic. If Dan tried to entice her into his bedroom she would…she would have to say no. There was still so much unanswered between them.

She was searching her undies drawer in the section she'd designated for her bikinis. There they were! Three little bikinis from her last holiday in the Greek islands, well worn, stretched by the salt water and faded by the sun. If only she'd bought something new! But, then, she hadn't known she was going to meet up with Dan.

But going to the beach was about pleasing young Josh, she told herself sternly. It's not about looking good for Dan. Who was she trying to convince? She didn't have to look seductive, just fairly attractive. Being totally incapable of making a decision, she stuffed all three bikinis into her large canvas bag, along with a towel.

Dan had told her they would make an early start and have breakfast on the beach so she actually had time to tidy up her little domain before her phone rang at the agreed time.

'I'm down at the front entrance.'

Mmm, how wonderful to hear his voice again after what had seemed ages! She cleared the frog from her morning throat but her voice still sounded a bit croaky when it actually came out.

'I'm on my way.'

The hospital was quieter than usual as she hurried downstairs from the doctors' quarters through the covered walkway that led towards the front entrance. When she arrived, she found that Dan had managed to park close to the door. Josh was leaning out through the open window of the car.

'Anita! Come and sit in the back with me.'

Dan opened the car door for her.

She smiled up at him, noting the happy, relaxed expression on his face. The casual cotton trousers and polo shirt made him look much younger today. He bent down and gently brushed his lips across her cheek.

'Good morning, Anita.'

All very casual, all very Sunday morning not on duty—especially for anyone who might be watching from the hospital.

Josh was leaning across the back seat, holding his arms out for a hug. She climbed in. Dan strapped Josh into his seat, closed the door and got into the driving seat.

She was immediately enveloped in an enthusiastic hug that smelt of pineapple and papaya, she couldn't decide which.

'Be careful of your sticky hands, Josh. Wait

until… Ah, too late. Sorry, Anita. Josh was too hungry to wait for breakfast so I put some pine-apple and papaya in a bag for him.'

'Don't worry, it was worth it for the welcome hug. I've got some moistened tissues in my bag.' She began feeling in the depths. 'Here they are! How about I do your hands first and then mine, Josh?'

'OK. There's some pineapple left in the bag if you want it, Anita.'

'No, thank you, Josh. I think I'll wait till breakfast now.'

'Do you want some, Daddy?' Josh was holding out his hands for Anita to clean them.

'No, thanks, Josh,' Dan said as he drove out through the hospital gates.

Josh chattered happily all the way to the beach. At one point, Anita realised that Dan was looking in his rear-view mirror.

'Everything OK back there?'

'Fine! Josh is explaining what we're going to do when we get there.'

'Oh, good. I'm glad you're not getting bored.'

'I don't think Josh would ever allow me to be bored.'

'You certainly seem to have taken to Anita, haven't you, Josh?'

Josh tried to lean forward but the straps in his specially constructed car seat restrained him.

'What do you mean, Daddy?'

'I mean you like Anita, don't you?'

'Of course I do! She's one of my bestest friends. You like her as well, don't you, Daddy?'

'Of course. She's one of my best friends.'

'We're here!' Josh shouted.

Anita, sinking lower in her seat, was glad this line of conversation had come to an abrupt end.

'Look, Anita! There's the sea and the beach! Oh, I do love coming to the beach with Daddy—and with you now! That makes it even betterer. Absolutely best!'

'Stay still until Daddy stops the car,' Anita said, putting one hand across to restrain the exuberant Josh.

As soon as Dan switched off the engine in the parking area beside the beach, Anita undid Josh's seat belt and allowed him to scramble out through the door.

'I can help you carry the stuff, Daddy.' Josh stood beside his father as the boot was unloaded.

Josh took his small rucksack and ran ahead. Anita slung her canvas shoulder-bag over her arm and Dan brought the remainder of the things in a large sports holdall.

As they walked along together she felt Dan take her hand. The gesture hardly registered with her as she linked her fingers through his just like old times. As she realised what she'd done she looked straight ahead, not daring to make eye contact. It was so easy to fall back into the way they had been. Perhaps it meant nothing to Dan, but it was a giant step for her. She asked herself what kind of useless resistance she was using to prevent herself falling hook, line and sinker for this man all over again.

None whatsoever at the moment! But did it really matter if she just allowed herself to enjoy being with him for one day? This warm ambience that existed between them was better

than the emotional turmoil she always experienced when she tried to analyse what had
happened when they'd split up. She was going
to live for the day!

What was that old saying her grandmother had
taught her when she'd been very small? The past
is over, forget it; the future hasn't happened so
don't worry about it; but the present is happening now so make the most of it.

'You're very quiet, Anita.'

'I'm just enjoying being back on the beach…
I mean…it's so lovely here. I used to come here
when I was a child.'

She reached down and pulled off her flip-
flops so that she could feel the sand between
her toes as she walked. 'Mmm, warm sand
between my toes, sun on my face—what more
can a girl ask for?'

Lots more, said the wicked little voice in her
head, very much aware that Dan had taken hold
of the hand that wasn't holding the flip-flops. She
glanced sideways and saw the gentle smile on his
face as he raised his face up towards the sun.

'Did your parents bring you here?'

'Yes. My amah brought me after my parents died.'

'So you were young when your parents died?'

She swallowed hard. It still hurt when she remembered the awful news being broken to her. 'They were killed in a car crash when I was ten. I'd been staying in England with my grandmother in the school holidays and I'd just returned to India. My mother's sister came out after my parents died and I was allowed to stay on here in India for a while before she had to return to England. It had been decided that I should go and live with my grandmother so she took me back with her.'

'That must have been hard for you.'

'Oh, it was! I was missing my parents. And England seemed so cold, especially in the winter at the boarding school I went to. Oh, how I missed the beach out here!'

She quickened her pace to a run for the sheer joy of being here again with the man she knew she had loved ever since she'd met him. He held onto her hand and joined in the run. At this precise moment, she felt she could forgive him anything.

'Dan, look at Josh! He's gone straight into that shack. You've obviously been here before.'

'Oh, we often have breakfast here on Sunday mornings. Just watch the way the waiters fuss over him.'

By the time they'd reached the wooden shack which was built on sturdy wooden supports above the sand, Josh was sitting at a table, sipping a freshly squeezed orange juice.

'May I have one of those?' Anita asked one of the waiters as he walked past.

He nodded and brought her one on his return.

She sipped at the deliciously cold drink as she looked out to sea. 'I'm on dolphin watch, Josh. Have you seen any this morning?'

'No, but we saw one last time we were here, didn't we, Daddy?'

'We did indeed. It gave us a good performance, really showing off how it could leap in the air out of the waves. Shouldn't be long before he comes along again. I've got a dolphin feeling.'

'When Daddy gets a dolphin feeling, they always start coming. You watch, Anita. It's just like magic when—There! Did you see it?'

'I did! And again. There he is again—And another one!'

'Two dolphins now!'

Anita thought that it was almost as if the dolphins had decided to give them a superb show.

'Do they know we're watching them, Daddy?'

'Oh, I'm sure they do! They don't put on a show like that for just anybody. What do you think, Anita?'

'Well, they've probably heard there's a famous surgeon visiting today so they'll pull all the stops out.'

'Are you famous, Dad?'

'Daddy's famous in his own field, Josh,' Anita said.

'What field?' Josh glanced around him. 'You mean beach, don't you, Anita?'

Josh laughed. 'I'm famous on the beach today and that's why the dolphins are doing their clever stuff. Why don't we order our breakfast now?

How do you like your eggs, Anita? No, don't tell me, let me try and remember…'

'Have you two had breakfast together before?'

'A long time ago, and I remember now that Anita could never make up her mind.'

She looked across the table at him and her heart felt as if it would burst.

'I'll go and tell the waiters what we want,' Josh said, getting down from his chair. 'Dad and I like scrambled eggs—is that OK with you, Anita?'

She nodded. It was as if time had suddenly stood still and she was miles away, back in London, back in those wonderful days of their affair. She swallowed hard as she saw the expression in Dan's eyes.

He reached for her hand. 'So many memories.' His voice was husky.

She curled her fingers around his. 'Too many memories.'

'No, there can never be too many. Remember that time I made you pancakes for breakfast because we'd only got one egg?'

She smiled. 'And then you chucked one of them up to the ceiling trying to toss it from the pan.'

'And it stuck…'

'Before it dripped down on the floor—'

'So we had to make do with toast. And I was starving hungry because—'

'Shh!' Anita warned as Josh came running back to the table.

'Why were you starving hungry, Dad?'

Dan's eyes twinkled at the memory of the strenuous night he'd spent with Anita all those years ago. 'Oh, I've forgotten now, Josh. What about you, Anita?'

'Long time ago. Before you were born, Josh.'

'That's why I haven't known you very long, Anita. I'm glad you came back to be Daddy's friend.'

'So am I,' Dan said quietly.

A waiter was coming across with a huge serving dish of scrambled eggs, followed closely by another waiter carrying toast and butter. Coffee came next and then a large bowl of papaya, pineapple and oranges.

The dolphins moved away while they were having breakfast. Occasionally, as they glanced up from their plates, they could be seen going further and further down the coast until they were completely out of sight.

Anita and Dan sat for a short while after breakfast simply looking out to sea. Only the sound of the waves hitting the shore disturbed their companiable silence. Josh had begun to play in the sand at the front of the shack. He was trying to construct some kind of castle, calling out occasionally to ask when they were going to help him.

Dan stood up. 'I'd better go and show willing. A bit of quality time, digging.'

Anita smiled. 'You're a good father.'

A concerned expression flitted across Dan's face. 'Do you think so? My father gave me quality time—when he wasn't working all hours, trying to be a successful businessman in Mumbai and going off for weeks at a time. My mother was something of a social butterfly, always in demand at charity fundraising lunches and other time-consuming events. I didn't see much of her when I was growing up. So I really don't know what a normal family life is like—you know, two parents spending whole days with—'

He broke off. 'Sorry, I didn't mean to bore you.'

'It's good to hear about your childhood. I remember you told me your parents had bought a house in Australia for their retirement. Are they still there?'

'Yes, they're enjoying life out there.' He was watching Josh with a fond expression.

Anita stood up. 'I'll come and help you with the castle. It's going to be too hot to dig soon.'

'I know. We'll need to be under the palm trees in the middle of the day unless…' He paused. 'I think perhaps we should return to the house and have a siesta. Josh always sleeps for a couple of hours in the early afternoon when he gets back from school.'

'Daddy, are you both coming to play with me?'

'Yes. We're on our way.'

Dan hurried ahead, turning as they reached the wooden steps leading down to the sand.

'So, will you come back to the house with us?'

She hesitated. The sensual warmth in his tone gave away exactly what he had in mind and the emotion in his eyes spoke volumes. It was what he hadn't said that was so tempting.

'Well, in view of the temperature we've already reached,' she began whimsically.

'So early in the morning,' he continued, a slow smile spreading over his handsome face as they walked across the sand towards Josh. 'And more heat to come, I believe.'

'Are you absolutely sure about that?'

'No doubt about it, Anita. We can't take the risk of sunstroke.'

'Well, in that case…'

'You can have this spade, Anita,' Josh said, grabbing her hand.

They all continued making the castle, casting off their layers of clothing as the heat rose during the morning. After a while Anita unpeeled her jeans and put them on her clothes pile. Her bikini didn't look out of place on the sandy beach as she announced her intention of going for a swim to cool off.

'Wait for me, Anita!' Josh, still partially clad, stood up. Anita pulled off his T-shirt so that he was ready to run with her in his little swim trunks.

Dan was last in the race to the sea because he hadn't put his trunks on and couldn't initially find them as he searched in his large holdall.

'Come on, Daddy,' Josh shouted as he and Anita made it to the water's edge.

As Dan finally located his swimming gear he glanced down to the shallows where his son was cavorting with Anita. He felt a swell of emotion rising up inside him. There was the woman he should have married, the woman who would have been mother to his child. The past should have been so different, he thought as he wrapped a towel round him and shrugged into his trunks.

But it wasn't too late to change things... With a loud whoop of excitement he ran down to the sea to join the two people in the world he loved the most.

CHAPTER SIX

'JOSH is fast asleep, whacked out with all that swimming, I think,' Dan said as he was coming through to the veranda from the sitting room. Anita watched him walking towards her with that easy gait, that loose athletic movement she'd always admired. Her spirits, which had been on a high all morning, moved up another notch. She hadn't expected to find such exhilaration in her new life here. This new-found euphoria was totally transitory. She accepted that, but at this moment she was willing to face the let-down when it came…because it inevitably would if she embarked on a relationship with Dan again. She didn't even know how he stood with his ex-wife, or what would happen when Rachel arrived.

He sank down among the cushions beside her.

She placed the large glass of icy water she'd been drinking on to a small side table. Since arriving back from the beach a few minutes ago, she'd simply been sitting still, recovering from the activities of the morning whilst enjoying the cool breeze from the fan above her head.

'You promised me a bath to get rid of all this sand,' she said, lifting up one bare foot to demonstrate what remained of the beach between her toes.

'Don't move!' Dan pretended to look shocked. 'You can't walk through the house like that. I don't want sand everywhere! I'll carry you.'

'Dan, no! I mean, do you really think you should?'

He raised one eyebrow. 'I always used to carry you. As I recall, you're as light as a feather.'

Before she could protest he'd scooped her up into his arms. 'You haven't put on any weight at all.'

She laughed. 'Yes, but you're older than you were, don't forget. All this he-man stuff is for younger men.'

'Nonsense! Stop trying to demolish my ego! Anyway, not yet forty. I work out at the gym…run on the beach when I can find the time…'

He was walking quickly through the sitting room with her in his arms, towards the hall and then up the stairs, as if to prove the point.

He was just so fabulously sexy when he was flexing his masculinity! She leaned her head against his chest. 'I'm not complaining. I'm loving every moment.'

Had she really dared to tell Dan that she was loving something they were doing together? The next thing she would be saying would be that she still loved him. No, that would be a step too far even for her runaway tongue…even if it was true…which it wasn't, of course… Oh, why couldn't she simply enjoy the moment?

She glanced up at Dan but he was concentrating on the last step of the stairs. She gave a sigh of relief that they'd made it. Yes, she really was loving it, trying to live for each precious moment without any thought of where they were heading emotionally. She found it so romantic to be carried upstairs again by Dan. How long had it been since that had happened? Oh, did it really matter? It was happening now and that was all she cared about.

She closed her eyes, feeling totally blissful as she often had when they'd been together before… before the split came… Don't think about it! Remember how romantic their life had been, how each time they'd met, each time their fingers had touched as they'd greeted each other, a frisson of excitement had run through her and the excitement of their relationship had started up again.

He was carrying her along the landing. She opened her eyes and saw that they were heading straight past the guest suite door and on towards Dan's own bedroom… She found she was holding her breath as he pushed open the door and carried her through to his bathroom.

She caught a brief glimpse of his domain, but it was enough to decide that his bedroom suite was equally as palatial as the guest suite. But it held that indefinable masculine touch to denote who slept there. Large antique mahogany wardrobe, acres of bookshelves, the bed still rumpled from where he'd slept in it the night before and clothes scattered over antique arm-chairs… But they'd reached the bathroom door. He was only slightly out of breath…must be in good shape with all that working out at the gym. She shivered with anticipation…

He put his foot against the bathroom door and pushed. A deliciously aromatic scent pervaded the bathroom and as she looked at the enormous bath she saw there was freshly scented water in it and rose petals floating on the surface. Oh, how romantic!

'You've run the bath for me!'

'For both of us.'

He deposited her gently onto a large towel spread over the floor. Then he lay down beside her and drew her into his arms.

'Are you ready…for the bath, I mean…?'

She opened her mouth to reply but her words were lost as he kissed her. She clung to him. There was a flurry of arm movements. She couldn't work out whose arm belonged to who as they tore at each other's clothes in a desperate rush to experience skin against skin, naked body against naked body. She could feel that Dan wanted to take her there on the floor but he was deliberately trying to hold off so that it would prolong the rapturous anticipation. His breath was ragged as he suddenly pulled away from her.

And in that moment she was way back in the past, getting ready to go to bed with Dan in their tiny, shower room, in that minuscule London apartment near the hospital. Their eyes locked in a knowing look. She knew that he was feeling something similar…pure heart-rending nostalgia. It was so easy to slip back into the way they had been when they'd lived together.

Why should she resist the temptation to believe that life wasn't so different now to how she'd perceived it when she'd been with him before? They'd never had rose petals in their shower. But they'd massaged bath lotions and oils over each other's skin…always preparatory to going to bed and making love. She knew where this romantic scene was heading…

He grasped her with his suntanned, muscular arms and lifted her over the side of the bath. She lay back in the scented water and gave herself up to the heady sensation of being seduced. But as she felt the deep sensual longing inside her body she knew that no effort was needed from Dan to make this seduction successful. She was there already simply by being close to him. But she wanted to hold back for a while, to savour each precious moment, so she was trying to keep the mood light for as long as possible.

'I'm glad you had the taps fitted in the middle of the bath, Dan.'

She raised her head from the scented bubbles around her and looked along the length of the enormous bath to the opposite end. Dan's head was just visible above the foam.

'And I had it made big enough for two.'

'So do you have parties here?'

Her tone was whimsical—she was trying to pretend that she was the only woman in his life at the moment which, of course, couldn't possibly be true. A man like Dan, superbly

handsome, successful in his medical career—
and single!—must have women drooling over
him all the time. She'd seen the female medical
staff in hospital falling over themselves to give
him the sort of attention that was way over and
above the call of duty.

Dan gave her a wicked smile. 'Parties? Oh, all
the time, but not every night. It would get boring.
Variety is the spice of life, don't you think?'

He slid one foot further forward and placed it
between hers, moving it slowly up to her knee
before raising himself from the depths of the
scented foam and reaching out to draw her into
his arms. She gave up trying to hold back as she
capitulated totally. How could she possibly resist
and what would be the point? It was as if her
bones had turned to jelly. She reached her hands
around his neck and drew his head towards hers
so that they were close, oh, so close, cocooned
in this scented paradise.

And then he kissed her, gently, his lips
blending with hers so that she felt as if she would
melt inside him. His hands were caressing her

body, gently at first and then with a more fierce passion. She arched her back, moving closer, ever closer, moulding her limbs around his to accommodate him. As she felt him enter her she groaned with the ecstatic sensations that were running through her.

'Yes, yes…oh, yes!'

She realised that the disembodied voice she could hear was her own. She hadn't been aware that she'd made any sounds at all. Everything was involuntary now. She moved in harmony with her man as he thrust deeper inside her. She belonged to him, always had done.

As she woke up, she felt the dawning of realisation of where she was. In Dan's exquisite bed, between rumpled cotton sheets in the middle of the afternoon, with no clear recollection of how she'd got here, but with that wonderful sensation of having made love for a lengthy period of time.

She turned her head on the pillow and felt a pang of disappointment as she saw she was alone. Yes, she could hear Dan splashing around in the bathroom. And then she remembered that Josh was somewhere just along the landing in his bedroom. She ought to get up but her languid limbs didn't want to leave this fabulous bed or shake off the sensations of being well and truly satisfied. She would like to stay on longer in this comfy nest, revelling in the aftermath of their lovemaking, but she had to return to the real world.

Glancing at the bedside clock, she could see that it had been almost two hours since Dan had told her that Josh was asleep. She really should get up so that if she heard him calling out she could go along to his room and reassure him that he wasn't alone.

The bedside phone rang. She called Dan and he appeared in the bathroom doorway wrapping a towel around himself. He blew her a kiss as he sprinted towards the phone.

'Could be the hospital. They have me on standby for Sunday evenings. Samaya always comes back to take care of Josh so...' He grabbed the phone and answered it.

'Who did you say you are?' He was frowning as he sprawled back on the bed, one hand fixing the towel while the other clasped the phone.

'Professor Crawford? I'm sorry. I don't know who gave you my number but...'

He was listening now as peals of girlish laughter came from the phone. 'Rachel? Well, why didn't you say so...? Well, yes, I know that's your name but I just hadn't made the connection. And you sounded so—well, professorlike. You had me totally fooled... Yes, of course I know you're really a professor... Listen, you've caught me at an awkward time.'

He was glancing sideways at Anita, who had become very still. As she swung her legs round to the side of the bed and stood up she felt a sudden chill running through her. And she knew it had nothing to do with the fact that Dan had lowered the temperature of the air-conditioning when they had both been at fever pitch during their love-making.

The woman on the phone was Rachel, his ex-wife, the mother of his child. The woman in

Dan's life that Anita had hoped never to see. Dan had intimated that his relationship with Rachel had been totally different to the one that she and Dan had experienced. But they seemed to have an easy friendship, judging by the way they were talking now. In fact, it sounded more than friendship…or was she reading too much into this? Either way, she didn't want to stay and hear Dan chatting to Rachel.

She pulled herself up out of the bed and lifted a damp towel off the floor where it had fallen when Dan had carried her into bed before their love-making—which now seemed as if it had been a dream. The sort of dream that had haunted her so often in the early days after their split when she'd felt as if she couldn't go on living without him. She padded across the carpet, her body tensing as she heard Dan laughing in what sounded to her like a conspiratorial way. She felt totally excluded, redundant in this family unit of mother, father and child.

Rachel had shared more with Dan than she had—marriage, conception, childbirth, the joy of seeing the child they'd produced together…and what else that she didn't know about?

OK, she admitted to herself that she was in danger of turning into a green-eyed monster if she continued to think like this, but what other conclusion was she to draw as she listened to Dan positively enjoying his conversation with his ex-wife?

She drew in a breath and tried to calm herself as she went into the bathroom. She'd been ecstatically happy in here only a short while ago and now…well, now she didn't know what she felt. She closed the door so she couldn't hear his voice or the peals of laughter that had just erupted over the phone again. Rachel sounded very young to be a professor. Young, carefree— what did she want? To resume a relationship with her ex-husband? Finally make claim to their little boy?

She stepped into the still warm bath. The suds had sunk a bit lower, along with her spirits—a lot lower! She'd been so stupid to imagine that Dan was hers, again, even for a moment, but, then, that was one of her faults. She was too trusting—she always went with her heart and not her head.

She added some more bubble bath from the fancy-looking glass bottle on the side of the bath and gave the water a big shake-up.

She was so intent on what she was doing she didn't hear him coming into the bathroom.

'Ah, more bubbles! Now, where were we?'

How could he be so nonchalant? She watched as he dropped his towel and stepped into the bath. She turned on her side so that she couldn't possibly be aroused by his athletic physique. The muscles in his legs had always got her going but, no, not now! It would be better if she climbed out and made it quite clear how she felt about him. She would do just that…in a moment when she felt she could make her point to best advantage.

She lay very still, her back towards him, but he pulled her closely against him so that they were now lying spoon-shaped at Anita's end of the bath. She tensed as she felt his hands around her.

It was definitely time for her to make it quite clear how she felt about the situation.

'So what did Professor Rachel want?' she asked.

'She's decided to arrive earlier than scheduled so that she can spend some time with Josh.'

'Oh, has she?'

Somehow Anita found the strength to pull herself away and climb out of the bath. Grabbing a particularly large fluffy towel from the enormous pile on the bathroom shelf, she enveloped herself entirely, even her hair, and sat down on a chair at the other end of the bathroom, glowering at the infuriating man in the bath. At least, that was the expression she was trying to make…but would he even notice her displeasure?

Dan sat up, wiping the suds from his face, baffled by the expression on her face. 'What did I say?'

'It's not what you said, it's what you didn't tell me about your relationship with Rachel that's the problem. I mean, do you think it's OK for Rachel to opt out of her child's life until he's almost six years old and then come rushing back on a mere whim, on the…?'

She searched for the right words to explain how she felt as she watched the uncomprehending expression spreading across Dan's face.

'On the flimsy excuse that just because she's got some work to do at the university, she'll pick up where she left off when she gave birth to her baby and get to know him again—perhaps resume her…her relationship with the man who fathered him.'

Dan opened his mouth to speak but Anita was in full flight and got there first.

'Tell me, Dan, are you happy with that?'

'Anita, she was suffering from postnatal depression when she opted out, as you put it.'

He pulled himself out of the bath, folding a towel around him and sitting at the other end of the bathroom.

'But she obviously recovered enough to climb the career ladder and become a professor, much sought after in the international field of medicine.'

'Surgery, actually,' he said quietly.

'Whatever!'

She raised both hands in a deprecating gesture then quickly withdrew them to the safety of her towelling touch-me-not cloak.

'I was speaking in the general meaning of the word,' she added in a deliberately pedantic tone of voice.

'Look, don't let's quarrel about this,' Dan said soothingly. 'Rachel will be arriving in a few weeks and she'll have a couple of weeks to spare before she has to give her lectures at the university. A couple of weeks in which she'll have time to get to know Josh. And for the record, I've no desire to resume any relationship other than the platonic, friendly relationship that usually exists between civilised ex-partners when they are joint parents of a child.'

Anita swallowed hard as she thought of all the implications. She'd better not alienate Dan any further by showing him how intensely jealous she was of this woman. She had to be sensible about it. Sensible? When had she ever been sensible where Dan was concerned?

With as much dignity as she could muster, she picked up her clothes from the floor and began to drag them on. She'd dressed in front of Dan more times than she could remember but she felt intensely aware of his presence this time. He'd even averted his eyes, showing that whatever rapport they'd established between them was now well and truly shattered.

A little voice was calling out from the bedroom. 'Daddy, where are you?'

Dan leapt up from his chair and reached for his clothes.

'I'll look after Josh,' Anita said calmly as now fully clothed, she went out through the door into the bedroom.

Josh was standing by the bed looking a bit lost. His eyes lit up when he saw her.

'Anita! I hoped you hadn't gone back to the hospital. Samaya is in the kitchen, making some of her little cakes for us. Will you come down and eat some with me? Will you stay for tea?'

She hesitated. The expectant, pleading expression on Josh's face softened her mood completely. How could she possibly decline such an invitation from this dear little boy? This wonderful child who'd never known what it was like to have a real mother to take care of him.

'I'd love to, Josh.'

'Good! Where's Daddy?'

'He's going to be down soon. We'll go on ahead.'

As she took his hand and went towards the landing with him she told herself she mustn't be judgmental about the part that Rachel had or hadn't played in Josh's life.

Dan had cared for him well, been father and mother to him, and Samaya had filled in all the gaps when Dan had been working. But, still, it had been hard for the boy to have had no permanent mother figure. But Dan obviously still had some feelings for Rachel and she couldn't change that.

Josh's little hand was still in hers as they walked down to the kitchen. It was good to know that the little boy's friendship with her was unconditional, whereas she didn't know where she was with his father! The only way she could continue seeing him was to be on her guard until she knew more.

Josh ran ahead into the kitchen. 'Samaya, Anita is going to stay for tea. Isn't that lovely? Have you baked enough cakes?'

'How many cakes would you like, Josh?' Samaya said as she lifted a fresh batch out of the oven.

Josh started counting the cakes on the oven tray. 'Eight, nine, ten. That should be enough with the ones you've baked already.'

The amah smiled across at Anita. 'I'll bring some cakes out to the pagoda in the garden. Dan always takes his tea there on Sundays before he has to go out again—either to the hospital or whatever social engagement he's arranged. Is Dan…is he coming down soon?'

Anita smiled back. 'Yes, he'll be down shortly. I'll take Josh out into the garden.'

'I'll come with you,' Dan said breathlessly as he hurried into the kitchen.

Minutes later they were all settled in the beautiful open-sided pagoda with the scent of roses and frangipani wafting in on the early evening sea breeze.

'It's so terribly English, having tea in the garden,' Anita said as she looked across the slatted teak table towards Dan.

She was making a deliberate effort to be ultra-polite, nothing more, just enough to tell Dan that she wasn't going to continue their earlier discussion about Rachel—well, not in front of Josh anyway.

'Daddy, may I go and ask Samaya for some more pineapple juice? It's all gone.'

'Yes, of course.'

Josh scampered away across the grass and disappeared into the house.

Dan put down his tea cup and reached a hand across the table in a conciliatory gesture. For an instant she hesitated before putting a hand across and touching his fingers. He leaned forward to clasp her hand.

'Truce?' He looked at her with that little-boy expression that had always melted her heart.

'When is she coming?'

Dan grinned. 'You're jealous, aren't you?'

'Well, of course I'm jealous!'

The words slipped out before she had time to think. And she was trying to be so cool!

Dan stood up and came round the table. 'You've got absolutely nothing to be jealous about.'

'Dan, it's not as if we're a couple again. Don't assume that just because we've been to bed again that means we're back where we were. There are so many reasons now why we can't put the clock back and start again.'

He leaned down and drew her to her feet, holding her against him. 'But it feels so right when we're together. I've dreamed of this, Anita.'

She felt the tears springing to her eyes. It did feel right but she couldn't bear it if everything ended again. She couldn't take another catastrophic disappointment like last time. Once she had met this Rachel woman, assessed the opposition, found out something of what had gone on in the past…

'Anita, can't you just enjoy what's going on between us now, instead of thinking about what happened in the past?'

She looked up into his eyes and felt her resolve weakening again. 'I'll try.'

He bent down and kissed her gently on the mouth. Anita felt as if he was sealing their relationship with this kiss and she knew this was how it was going to be for the foreseeable future. At least until after Rachel had gone away again…or if she'd decided she was going to stay on or even take Josh away with her…

'What if Rachel wants to take Josh with her?' she asked. 'I know you said she gave you custody of him when he was a baby but she may wish to change that now he's older.'

'I don't think she will.'

'But when she sees how adorable he is…'

'Talking of which,' Dan said as he watched his son charging back across the lawn, 'careful with the juice, Josh, you're spilling it! Perhaps we'll finish this conversation another time when—'

Dan's mobile rang. 'Yes, Sister… I'll be with you right away…'

Josh had climbed up onto Anita's knee. He reached up and whispered in her ear. 'Daddy's talking to the hospital. That means he'll be going back to work this evening. Will you have to…?'

'There's been a major incident further down the coast,' Dan said. 'A capsized passenger boat. We're taking some of the casualties straight into A and E so every available medic is needed. Will you help out, Anita?'

She looked down at the wistful little face so close to hers.

'Josh…'

'It's OK, Anita. I'm used to Daddy having to go back to hospital so I'll get used to you going with him. When I'm a lot bigger I'll be a doctor and I can come as well.'

'That's the spirit!' Dan lifted up his son from Anita's lap and ruffled his hair affectionately.

'We'll be back as soon as we can,' Dan said.

'Josh, I'll be staying back at the hospital when I go off duty,' Anita said gently, feeling it her duty to set the record straight so that both father and son—in their different ways—knew what to expect tonight.

She noted a brief flickering of expression as Dan listened but he made no comment. Josh reached across and gave Anita a big kiss on the cheek. 'Come and see me again soon, won't you?'

'I'd love to.'

'We'd better go,' Dan said as he set off towards the house, still carrying Josh. 'Sister sounded a bit harassed.'

Samaya was clearing up the kitchen but she dried her hands on a towel as soon as she saw Josh and reached out to take him from Dan.

'Come on, Josh. What game shall we play this evening?'

'How about chess, Samaya?'

Samaya smiled. 'Yes, you beat me last time but this time…'

'I'm teaching Josh to play chess and he's learning very quickly,' Dan explained as they hurried out to the car. 'Samaya is very kind to him when they play together but I'm sure he really will beat her soon.'

'A bright boy. As I said before, you've done an excellent job of bringing him up. Have you told him his mother is coming to see him?'

'Not yet.' Dan started the engine and began to drive towards the open gates. 'When I heard that

Rachel was coming to give some lectures at the university I thought it was too early to tell Josh. I thought it better to wait until it actually happened. I mean, she might change her mind or…or anything…'

'Is she prone to changing her mind?'

Dan stared ahead, a hard expression on his face. 'In my experience…in the little time I knew her… Look, why don't we change the subject and concentrate on the work ahead of us?'

CHAPTER SEVEN

THE patients were being wheeled in on trolleys as Dan and Anita arrived in A and E. Anxious relatives crowded around. From the brief details Anita had gathered from the most coherent patients and relatives, she discovered that there had been a family party of local people on board a two-tiered cruiser. They had been watching the dolphins leaping out of the sea and too many people had rushed to one side of the boat on the top tier at the same time. The boat had capsized, spilling many people into the water.

'Two people are missing but the coastguards are still searching,' Dan told Anita. 'One patient has been confirmed dead on arrival. The paramedics are working on another seemingly lifeless young woman in the end cubicle. Let's see if we can resuscitate her.'

As they went into the cubicle a tired paramedic straightened up and looked across the still body of his patient.

'I can't detect a pulse—'

'I'll take a look at her,' Dan interrupted as he anticipated the wailing sounds that were now coming from the woman's distraught boyfriend.

'Fatima! Fatima!' The man was weeping.

Dan turned the woman on her side, checking that there was a clear airway.

'There was water in the lungs initially, Doctor,' the paramedic explained. 'We've aspirated it all out but—'

'Hold on, there *is* a faint pulse,' Anita said, her fingers on the cold wrist of her patient.

Dan moved his patient back to a supine position and placed his stethoscope against her chest.

Moments passed before he raised his head and looked across at Anita. 'There's a new cardiac drug which worked on a similar patient last time I used it. Take her blood pressure again.'

Anita worked on her patient until Dan returned seconds later, carrying the required drug. He drew it up into a syringe and injected the contents. Time seemed to stand still as they stood over their patient, waiting for a reaction. Anita found she was holding her breath.

Suddenly their patient coughed. Anita checked the latest blood-pressure reading. From a very low pressure the reading was now approaching a much healthier situation.

Seconds later the patient opened her eyes.

'Fatima!' The young man sprang to his feet and moved back to the examination couch. 'Is she going to be all right, Doctor?' he asked Anita in rapid Hindi.

She replied in the same language. 'All the signs are that she is recovering. She is basically a strong, healthy woman but we will have to keep her here in hospital under observation until she fully recovers.'

'Of course, of course...'

Dan asked Anita to stay on and complete the necessary treatment of their patient while he moved on to a seriously ill patient in the next cubicle.

Half an hour later, having done all the necessary tests to ensure that she hadn't missed any symptoms, Anita had her patient transferred to a ward.

She moved straight on to the next patient, one of the crew members who'd injured his leg while swimming underwater to try to save one of the passengers.

'There was a woman trapped under the boat,' he told Anita in a variation of the Hindi language incorporating the local Rangalore dialect which she'd learned as a child. 'I tried to reach her but my leg caught in a narrow gap as I tried to go through. I wrenched it out and there was an awful pain near the top here. I think I passed out or something. When I came to I was floating on the top of the water.'

Anita took a pair of scissors and cut down the side of her patient's jeans. She didn't need an X-ray to form her diagnosis of a fractured femur. Fragments of the thigh bone were sticking out through the skin.

'The big bone at the top of your leg is fractured, Ahmed,' she told her patient. 'I'll get you to X-Ray and then we'll be able to treat it when we see exactly the extent of the injury.'

'OK, Doctor. Has the woman been brought up yet…the one I tried to save?'

Anita hesitated. She'd already been told the bad news. 'I'm afraid not,' she said gently. 'The boat has now sunk and the woman you were trying to save was still trapped underneath. A couple of experienced divers are down in the water but it's a recovery operation now.'

Ahmed swallowed hard and his eyes filled with tears. 'I wish I could have saved her. She was such a kind woman. I remember her on the boat, being so good with the children at the party. She…' He put a hand over his face as his voice choked. 'I wish…'

'You did all you could, Ahmed,' Anita said. 'You tried. That's all any of us can do. Sometimes…'

She had to stop speaking. 'Sometimes trying is not enough,' she'd been going to say, but for a few seconds she remained silent.

The porter and a nurse arrived to take Ahmed to X-Ray but Anita asked them to wait outside the cubicle for a couple of minutes. She needed more time to prepare her patient.

'Is everybody accounted for?' Anita asked Dan as they sat drinking tea in the much quieter main area of A and E.

Dan nodded. 'Three confirmed dead. One woman trapped in the wreckage, presumed dead. Ten people allowed home and the rest admitted.'

'The woman in the wreckage—have the divers located her?'

Dan nodded. 'They say she can't possibly be alive. The divers couldn't reach her because she's in an impossibly narrow space.'

'I know. One of my patients tried to get her out earlier and fractured his femur.'

'That was Ahmed, wasn't it? I took him to Theatre after his X-ray. The femur needed nailing at the top. When he'd been in Recovery for a while I found him a bed in the orthopaedic ward. He was concerned about the woman he couldn't save.'

'I know,' Anita said quietly, as she remembered how she'd had to comfort Ahmed before he'd gone to X-Ray. 'Totally selfless. Such a brave young man. Do you think he'll have any problems in the future with that leg?'

'Are you checking whether I did a good job, Doctor?'

Anita smiled.

'That's the first time you've smiled since you left my house.'

'Not much to smile about this evening, was there?'

'There were more survivors than victims.'

'Try telling that to the relatives of the victims.'

'Hey, don't let your work knock you out, Anita. You've got to move on or you'll be no use to the patients you deal with tomorrow.'

'Oh, I'll be fine by tomorrow when I've had a good night's sleep.' She stood up, deliberately removing the stethoscope from around her neck and carrying it in one hand to make her feel she really was off duty.

Dan stood up and put one hand on her arm to detain her. 'Don't rush off, Anita. How about I take you home for a nightcap, help you to really relax and bring you back in the morning, refreshed and—?'

'No, Dan!' She couldn't help smiling as she looked at the wicked way he was looking down at her. Something was already stirring deep down inside her but she intended to be firm. There were too many issues at stake here and she wanted to stay in control—for once.

'Do you really want to spend the night in the doctors' quarters? I've slept there occasionally and really…well, it's not conducive to relaxation. I mean, ambulances screaming through the night, hard narrow bed…'

'Dan, I don't want to talk about the real reason now—not here.' She lowered her voice as she glanced across at the cubicle from where a couple of night nurses were emerging, pushing newly set examination trolleys.

'It's the thought of Rachel coming out here, isn't it?' he said under his breath.

She nodded. 'We'll discuss it some other time.'

'If you came back with me tonight, we could discuss it then.'

She shook her head, this time sadly, because she could think of nowhere else she would like to be that night than Dan's house.

He raised his hands, palm upwards, in a gesture of resignation. 'OK, I know when I'm beaten. Sleep well.'

She turned and walked away quickly before she could change her mind and spend a whole night in Dan's bed...

For the next couple of days, as she worked with Dan she knew the mood of their relationship had changed again. At first she felt that was how it should be. That was what she needed to survive the next few weeks before Rachel arrived.

Dan was polite at the hospital but there were no further invitations. She threw herself into her work and tried to convince herself that it was all for the best. Until she'd seen Rachel she couldn't settle back into the relationship that had been developing between Dan and herself.

But the strain of this cooler relationship when they worked together was getting to her. So she was positively relieved to receive a summons to his office, via one of the nurses, at the end of the second day just as she was going off duty.

As she went along the corridor she felt apprehensive. At least they would be able to talk and clear the air.

He opened the door almost immediately and drew her inside, the cool approach he'd adopted during the last two days having vanished. She took a deep breath.

'Is this work or…?'

'I had to talk to you. Anita, I can't cope with this distance between us.'

'You've been totally unapproachable!'

'You turned me down flat on the night after the boat disaster. I wanted—'

'Dan, I know what you wanted. I wanted it, too, but there was the question of Rachel arriving soon and… When is she arriving?'

His eyes flickered. 'That's what I wanted to talk to you about. She phoned me here at the hospital. It's sooner than we thought. She arrives in four days' time. Can't wait to see Josh, she tells me.'

'Four days?' She moved away from him and sank down in one of the comfy chairs by the window.

He strode across and pulled the other chair nearer to her, sitting astride the arm, leaning forward so that they were very close. He placed his hands on either side of her shoulders.

Anita swallowed hard. 'I knew she was coming soon but now that it's imminent I—'

'Anita, it's no big deal.'

'No big deal! She's your ex-wife. She's Josh's mother, for heaven's sake!'

'And that's another thing. Josh misses you terribly. He keeps asking about you.'

'But you haven't invited me since…'

'You turned me down. I didn't think you wanted to come.'

'I was tired that night. Tired and confused about Rachel coming.'

'Well, will you come back with me tonight?'

'OK!' She surprised herself. 'I was going to make myself wait until I'd seen Rachel but…'

There! She'd shown her real feelings after two days of hiding them. She felt a sense of relief.

Dan gave her the wicked grin that always melted her heart. He stepped forward and drew her into his arms.

'I knew you'd come round if I left you alone for a while.'

'Dan, it's not good for me to live on this…this roller-coaster of emotions!'

'Well, why don't you give in? Come home with me tonight—if not for my sake, come home to see Josh. He's besotted with you—you know he is. And he's only a little boy. He doesn't understand the female sex any more than I do.'

She looked up into his eyes and felt her heart beating more rapidly.

'When you put on that wheedling voice, Dr Dan, you think you can twist me round your little finger.'

He ran his tongue over his lips. His eyes, gazing down at her, were twinkling with anticipation.

'So, are you well and truly twisted, Dr Anita?'

'I'm longing to see Josh again,' she said carefully.

'I'll take that as a yes.'

He lowered his head and kissed her gently. Their kiss deepened as she found her treacherous body moulding itself to the muscular bits of his body that she knew so well.

She moved in his arms and he loosened his embrace, looking down at her enquiringly.

'You're still not sure, are you?' he asked.

'I don't think I can be sure of anything until…until I know…' She searched for the right words. 'Until I know…'

'Until you've assessed what sort of a relationship is going on between Rachel and me?'

'Exactly!'

His hands tightened on her arms. 'You can be the most infuriating woman but in spite of that…' His voice was husky with emotion now. 'I can't help…'

She held her breath. Was he going to tell her he loved her? If he did, would she believe him—ever?

He leaned forward and kissed her again very gently at first, then with more pressure. She felt his arms enveloping her once more and sensed his body responding to the emotional rapport that was developing between them again. If only she could trust him as she once had! But she couldn't! Not yet. Until she knew beyond a shadow of a doubt that Rachel wasn't going to be a threat.

She leaned back from him in his arms and he released her, as if sensing the emotional turmoil she was experiencing.

He put a finger under her chin and tilted her face so that she had to look into his eyes. 'Let's go home,' he said gently.

She nodded.

For the next three days she went home with him every night. Looking back on it, as the fourth day dawned Anita decided it had been like a mini-honeymoon. Working together in total harmony during the day before enjoying an evening together. And then, after they'd both put Josh to bed, settling themselves for a candlelit supper for two, prior to going to bed and making love as often as they felt like it.

She turned her head to look at Dan's dark tousled hair on the pillow beside her. It had been worth capitulating and listening to her heart instead of her head. She'd grown so much closer to Dan. And she'd truly bonded with Josh. She felt as if he was her own flesh and blood...which wasn't a good way to feel on the morning that his birth mother would be arriving!

'Dan, I must go to the hospital,' she said.

He opened his eyes and a dreamy, sleepy smile hovered over his lips. He reached for her. She sighed as he took her into his arms again. What a night they'd had! The climactic excitement of their love-making had left her feeling utterly and completely in love with this man, but she had now to become practical again.

'I've got to work today.'

'You don't have to! I told you to take the day off so you can be here when Rachel arrives. I've got enough staff to cover for you.'

'Not a good idea.' She was already turning away, swinging her legs over the side of the bed.

'OK, but you'll come back this evening? The sooner you meet Rachel...'

'Yes, I will.' She was already heading for the bathroom.

'I'll drive you in,' he said, getting out of bed from the other side.

As she worked through the day in A and E she could feel her apprehension mounting about meeting Rachel. She was fully focussed on her work, but she was glad that most of it was fairly routine. Suturing wounds didn't require much expertise. Diagnosing fractures, having them X-rayed and applying casts were second nature to her. And there were no mysterious diagnoses to tax and worry her today.

All in all, a straightforward sort of day, she

thought as she went out through the front gates of the hospital and hailed a cab.

Sitting in the back of the cab, she looked out at the early evening scene, people scurrying along, anxious to get home, *tuk-tuks* weaving in and out of the traffic, the odd stray cow meandering home, miraculously missing the motorized vehicles that swerved to avoid it. She was going to the place where she most felt at home but she wouldn't stay the night. Snippets of the conversation she'd had with Dan as he'd driven her to the hospital that morning came back to her now.

She'd asked Dan if Rachel was going to stay at his house.

He'd seemed amused at the idea. 'No, of course not! I've booked her into the Leila Hotel.'

'I've heard it's very luxurious there.'

She'd kept quiet after that, not wanting to sound as jealous as she felt.

Dan had told her he needed to go to his office for a while and suggested she come with him so they could have coffee before she went into work. The strained atmosphere had returned with a vengeance as they'd both fallen silent, reviewing how they were going to deal with Rachel's arrival.

Anita had drunk her coffee quickly and then stood up, saying she was going to A and E. Dan had hurried to overtake her so that he could open the door. They'd stood together awkwardly in the door to the corridor while a couple of medical students had gone past, chatting and laughing together as if they hadn't a care in the world.

'Oh, to be young and irresponsible again!' Dan had said, watching the young men disappearing round the corner. 'If only we could turn the clock back and start again!'

'Knowing what we know now, with the benefit of hindsight, would you change anything?' she'd asked him.

'Of course I would! But we have to live life with what we've got now. And we can make it work, Anita. After you've met Rachel…'

'Let me meet her first and then I'll know what I'm up against!'

He raised an eyebrow. 'It's going to be fine. Believe me!'

If only she could!

'So you are the ex-girlfriend that Dan has been telling me about!'

Anita finished paying the driver of her cab in Dan's driveway and prepared to shake hands with the red-haired vision of sophistication who was advancing towards her from the house. She didn't look a bit like a professor! Long, shiny hair sitting on her shoulders, lovely tanned skin, fabulously cut white linen trousers and expensive-looking silk blouse.

But Rachel's voice was full of authority. Her whole demeanour was that of a person who was used to having deference shown to her. But Anita took the outstretched hand and received a firm grip.

Anita cleared her throat. 'How was the flight from America? Not too jet-lagged, I hope?'

'Oh, I did the long flight last week. I've just spent a few days in Goa at a fabulous hotel right on the beach—it's the sister hotel of the one I'm staying at here. I liked it so much I phoned Dan and asked him to make a reservation for me.'

'Where is Dan?'

'He was right behind me but he had a call on his mobile. Here he is. Dan, Anita's here?'

Dan came across the drive and kissed Anita on the cheek. 'Did you have a good day?'

'Uneventful,' she said quietly.

He walked ahead, as if unsure which woman he should be escorting. Anita hurried to keep up with him, not wanting to have to be alone with Rachel.

Rachel chatted in her mid-Atlantic accent. The initial impression that she was delivering a lecture had eased somewhat. Anita wondered if, like her, Rachel was feeling nervous. Bound to be! Meeting the ex-girlfriend of her ex-husband. How complicated! Anita thought how much she hated being referred to as the ex-girlfriend—though she wasn't sure what she was any more.

Josh was on the veranda, playing with his train set. He looked up as the grown-ups came in and launched himself at Anita.

'Anita, Daddy didn't tell me you were coming, did you, Daddy?'

'I wasn't sure if...' Dan broke off. 'Well, here we all are. This calls for champagne, I think.' He lifted the bottle out of the cooler on the table. 'We were waiting for you to arrive, Anita.'

'Yes, I couldn't get away.'

Not true! She wanted to spend as little time as she could in this cosy family set-up. After all, it was in Josh's interests that he be allowed to bond with his mother. She had to give them a chance for Josh's sake. If she hadn't loved the little boy so much she wouldn't have made the unselfish decision to give the family unit more time to themselves.

She'd wrestled with her conscience during last night while she'd lain awake, in between bouts of love-making, unable to sleep as she'd worried about the impending visit of Josh's mother. And she'd come to the conclusion that she should give the woman a chance. Rachel might be giving out an aura of self-confidence at the moment but Anita could see she was as apprehensive about the difficult situation as she was.

Dan was pouring champagne into three glasses and lemonade into a fourth glass for Josh.

Josh put his glass on the floor and immediately knocked it over as he reached for one of his trains. Anita leapt up and went to the kitchen for a cloth, glad of the excuse to escape.

Dan and Rachel were deep in conversation when she returned. Josh was happily playing around the lemonade puddle area. Anita got down on her knees and mopped up the pool before returning to the kitchen. She leaned against the sink. From the veranda she heard peals of laughter breaking out. Dan and Rachel obviously had a lot in common.

Very much ex. She rinsed and wrung out the cloth into the sink. She would have to return. She couldn't just disappear. Although, from the sound of things, would they notice?

She took a deep breath and headed back to the veranda, reaching immediately for her glass of champagne. Courage and decorum, that's what she needed!

Dan came across with the bottle to top up her

glass. He and Rachel had already finished theirs. His fingers touched hers as he moved away. A frisson of longing ran through her as she saw him returning to be with Rachel. This was how it would always be because there was a family bond between the two of them. Josh was the bond that would bind them together for ever.

And she shouldn't try to break that precious bond. She began to sip her champagne slowly.

'Let's have another game of chess, Josh,' Rachel said brightly. 'Stop playing with your trains and come up to the table here. I'll set out the pieces and—'

'I don't want to!'

Anita had never heard Josh speak so vehemently.

'Josh. It's good for you to stretch your mind. My father taught me chess when I was little—like you—and I used to play with him every evening.'

'I'm nearly six.'

'Well, there you are, then. You need to use your leisure time to full advantage, like I always did as a child.'

Josh got up from the floor and came over to Anita's chair, climbing onto her lap and leaning against her.

'I want to go out into the garden. Will you come with me, Anita?'

She was very much aware that Dan and Rachel were watching her. She stood up almost defiantly. 'Yes, I'd like to go outside as well. I need some air.'

She took the little boy's hand and together they walked out along the veranda, but not before she'd seen Rachel's eyes flashing with obvious disapproval.

'Supper's almost ready,' Dan called after her.

She stepped out into the rose-scented night, the tiny hand still clutching hers. As soon as she'd escaped the cloying atmosphere of the veranda she wanted to run like a child. Holding tightly to Josh's hand, she took him across the sparse dry grass towards the wall at the end of the garden. Together they climbed the wall and sat down, looking out towards the sea which was clearly discernible in the distance.

It was that magical time of the evening when twilight changed to darkness. The sun had disappeared into the sea, and the whole earth seemed still and at peace with itself. For a few minutes they simply sat quietly together, Josh leaning against her, occasionally looking around him if a bird flew near to settle in one of the trees nearby.

'I love this time of the day, don't you, Josh?'

The little boy smiled. 'I like being here with you, Anita.' He leaned forward and looked up into her eyes. 'Do I really have to like that lady?'

Anita swallowed hard. Oh, the poor little lamb! What an awful dilemma he was facing. Suddenly being confronted by a woman—a brilliant academic—who obviously hadn't got a clue about children.

'Rachel is your real mother, Josh,' Anita said carefully. 'She brought you into the world.'

'I know, but why did she leave me?'

'Well, she was very ill when you were a baby.'

'Yes, but she must have got better. So why didn't she come to find me before now? Why did Daddy have to—?'

He broke off as he saw Dan walking across the grass towards him.

'Daddy!'

Dan broke into a run, reaching out to his son and taking him in his arms. 'I came to tell you two that supper's ready.'

Josh snuggled up against his father. 'Anita's been telling me why Rachel couldn't look after me when I was a baby. But I don't understand why she couldn't have come sooner to meet me. Didn't she like me when I was a baby?'

Dan's eyes met Anita's over the little boy's head. She waited breathlessly for his reply.

'Of course she liked you…but there were problems…problems that grown-ups have and—'

'Oh, it doesn't matter,' Josh said, hugging Dan closer. 'As long as you and Anita like me.'

'We love you, Josh,' Dan said huskily as he looked once more at Anita.

She tried to find her voice but the emotion was too much for her. She got down from the wall and began walking back towards the house. How was she to resolve this situation? She wasn't Josh's real mother and never would be. Rachel had rights that would never be hers. As long as she stuck around she would be the fly in the ointment. She would prevent Josh from bonding properly with Rachel.

Not that she could blame the boy! If she'd been a child in the same situation, she'd have been as confused as he was.

'Are you OK, Anita?'

She assured Dan that she was as they walked back into the house.

Samaya had put out a large tureen on the dining-room table. Dan served the spicy vegetable soup into bowls.

'You're lucky to have such a good cook, Dan,' Rachel said. 'I've never had time to learn to cook. Maybe when I retire I'll give it a try.'

'Are you going to retire? How old are you, Rachel?' Josh said, chewing on a piece of home-made bread roll.

'Don't speak with your mouth full, Josh. But to answer your questions, I'm thirty-nine and I don't intend to retire for a long time yet. Perhaps I'll retire when I'm fifty-something so that I've got more time for travelling, which I love! Do you like travelling, Josh?'

'I like going to the beach.'

'Yes, I like going to the beach.' Rachel paused. 'Would you like to start calling me Mommy… or Mummy?'

'No, thank you,' Josh said quietly, as he pushed his soup bowl to one side.

There was an embarrassing silence for a few seconds. The tension was relieved when Samaya came in with a large serving dish of roast chicken.

Somehow Anita managed to get through the rest of the meal before announcing that it was time she went back to the hospital.

Josh asked her to stay so that she could put him in the bath and read him a story, just like she'd done for the last few nights.

'I can do that,' Rachel said, pushing back her chair from the table.

'Yes, of course you can,' Dan said. 'I'll call you a cab, Anita, and then I'll help you, Rachel.'

Josh got down from the table and took hold of Dan's hand possessively. 'Stay with me, Daddy.'

'I'm going to stay with you, Josh,' Dan said, before dialling on his mobile and ordering a cab.

Outside, he cupped her face with his hand, kissed her tenderly and thanked her for her understanding, for everything. He waved from the front porch, holding the clinging Josh in his arms as Anita was driven away.

She turned and watched them until the cab had gone through the gates. Oh, how she longed to stay on with both of them, to enjoy the unhurried childish pleasures of bathtime and stories that had meant so much to her in the previous days.

Tonight it was Rachel who was going to play happy families. Anita found herself hoping that Rachel would unbend a little and be kind to her little boy. Being a birth mother didn't necessarily mean that you knew how to look after the child you'd brought into the world.

She couldn't help feeling sorry for Rachel at the supper table when she'd invited Josh to call her Mummy. If that had happened to her, she would have been absolutely devastated. But it was early days and Josh may well warm towards his mother…if he was given a chance.

She asked herself once more if she was making the situation more difficult for mother and son to bond. And the answer she came up with was that she wasn't making it any easier.

So what was the solution? She loved Josh, she loved Dan and wanted to be with him. In an ideal world they would be a family unit.

The cab was turning in through the hospital gates. She would try to put her problems on hold for the moment.

CHAPTER EIGHT

A FEW days later, as Anita emerged from a cubicle in A and E, having just fixed a drip for a patient who'd been vomiting excessively, Anita was surprised to see Rachel walking into the department, a quietly subdued Josh by her side, carrying his school satchel. When she'd worked with Dan that morning he hadn't mentioned anything about this unexpected event.

Rachel was making a beeline for the nurses' station. Anita hurried across as she saw Rachel interrogating the nurses.

'But you must know where Dr Mackintosh is,' Rachel was saying imperiously.

'May I have your name, please?' Sister Razia said curtly.

'I'm Professor Crawford. I'm here to give a series of lectures at the university.'

'Ah, yes. I've heard about you, Professor. I'll try Dan's mobile again but—'

'Perhaps I can help,' Anita said.

'Anita!' Josh gave her a big smile. 'Everybody's trying to find Daddy.'

'He went up to Theatre to advise the surgeon about one of the patients he'd sent up, and the surgical team asked him if he would scrub up and give them a hand as he understood the case better than any of them. Perhaps I can help you, Rachel?'

Rachel smiled, displaying her flawlessly and obviously expensively maintained dazzling white teeth. Her red hair gleamed under the bright striplights above the nurses' station.

'I came to tell Dan I had the urge to pick up Josh from school and spend some quality time with him. Dan's mobile was on voicemail so I thought I'd just call in.'

She swung round to bestow the dazzling smile on Sister and the two nurses who were working with her.

'If any of you would like to come to my lectures, I'm sure it could be arranged. It's primarily for surgeons and surgical medical students but anyone attached to the hospital or the university can come. My first lecture is next week. It's on emergency surgery required in the accident and emergency department so I think you would find it relevant to your own personal career structures, don't you, Sister?'

'I'm sure it would be, Professor,' Sister Razia said quickly.

'Would you show me around your department, Sister? Perhaps I could leave Josh here with Dr Anita. They get on very well. He's going to be a surgeon when he grows up, you know, aren't you, Josh?'

'Maybe.'

Josh sneaked his little hand into Anita's.

'I'll give you a quick tour of the department, Professor,' Sister said. 'But if we get busy I'm afraid I'll have to leave you.'

'Thank you. Don't worry if you do have to go, I can wander around by myself. Perhaps you could start off by showing me your treatment rooms. I often find…'

'I'm going to take a break, Sister,' Anita said. 'I'll take Josh with me.'

Josh was clutching her hand as she headed for the corridor in the direction of the staff canteen.

'What would you like to drink and eat, Josh?' she said, as they stood in front of the glass-enclosed goodies at the counter.

'Orange juice in a box with a straw and one of those chocolate biscuits wrapped in paper with the elephants on it.'

They settled themselves at a table. Josh took a long suck on the straw and then smiled happily across at Anita.

'I'd like to be a doctor and drink orange juice like this every day.'

Anita laughed. 'We don't sit around all day, drinking orange juice and eating chocolate, you know. We have to work very hard.'

'Oh, I know that. I really would like to be a surgeon but Rachel keeps asking me about it and I wish she wouldn't.'

'I just think she's very proud of you because you're her son.'

'Funny, isn't it?'

'What is?' Anita said carefully.

'Me being Rachel's son. I mean, I don't know her at all, do I?'

'You're getting to know her. It takes time to get to know someone.'

'It was easy enough for me to get to know you, Anita.'

He paused to take another drink of his juice, put the carton carefully back on the table and looked up at her with wistful eyes.

'You see, I know when you're trying to teach me something…like telling me what a new word means…but you don't keep coming back to me and testing if I remember it, do you?'

'No, I don't. I'm not your schoolteacher so I only point things out that might interest you or if you ask me about something.'

'And that's OK! It's fun to learn things—but not all the time like when Rachel goes on and on about how important it is that I remember something because when I grow up—Oh, ever since she picked me up from school she's been trying to teach me things.'

'That's because she cares about you, Josh.'

'Well, you care about me but we just have fun together. Rachel starts telling me about when she was small how brainy she was at school. And when she got home her parents used to make her do her homework and now she's an accy—academic.'

Josh sniffed, took another drink and said, 'What's an academic, Anita?'

Anita suppressed a smile. She took hold of Josh's hand, the one that wasn't clinging to the drink as if he was afraid someone might take it away.

'An academic is somebody who is teaching or working in a university and they spend a lot of time reading, writing books and—'

'Does Rachel write story books I could read?' Josh's eyes flashed with interest.

'Well, no. Her books are usually very complicated and meant to be read by other academics.'

'That's a pity. You see, I'm really trying to like

her because Daddy must like her, mustn't he? Well, he used to be married to her and you have to like somebody to make a baby together, don't you?'

Anita swallowed hard as she worried about what this was leading up to. Yes, Dan must have felt something for Rachel to have produced this lovely child.

'Yes, the mummy and the daddy do have to have…er…a close relationship with each other.'

'That's what I thought. You see, my English teacher at school has to give us lessons on sex and stuff and she said the mummy and the daddy have to like each other and get very close to each other so that the daddy can plant a seed in the mummy's tummy. And then the baby pops out of the mummy's tummy after you wait a bit for it to grow and—Daddy!'

Dan had just walked in through the door, still in theatre greens, his mask hanging below his chin. Josh leapt up from his seat and ran between the tables to greet him.

'Hello, son.' Dan lifted Josh up into his arms before walking across to Anita's table.

'I had a garbled message from Sister and gathered this was where you would be.' He sat down on the chair next to hers, Josh on his lap.

'Where's Rachel?'

'Having a guided tour of the hospital. I've just had a message to say that Sister Razia from A and E has offloaded her onto Sister Banesa in Obstetrics. I don't know where she's going after that. Well she is something of a celebrity.'

'Obviously.'

'So why did Rachel collect Josh from school?'

'She wanted to spend some quality time with Josh,' Anita said.

Dan gave her a wicked grin. 'Well, I don't think she would approve of you feeding him chocolate biscuits during her quality time.'

'Daddy, I like being a doctor and eating chocolate biscuits.'

'So do I, Josh. I'm starving. But may I suggest we go back home—it's almost time for me to stop doctoring. We can have some tea at home and then Samaya will look after you while Rachel and I go out for dinner.'

He glanced across at Anita. 'Rachel has been invited to dinner at the Vice Chancellor's house and she's asked me to accompany her.' A worried expression crossed his face. 'I can't get out of it.'

'Dan, it's perfectly natural she would want you to go with her.'

'Why can't Anita look after me tonight, Daddy?'

'I don't know what Anita's plans are for the evening.'

Anita hesitated as she thought that once again she was reinforcing her own bond with Josh. And meanwhile the bond between mother and son just wasn't happening. But looking across the table at the pleading expression in Josh's eyes she knew she couldn't let him down.

Yes, as long as she was here, being maternal with him, he was never going to bond with his real mother and her feelings of guilt were growing by the minute. For the time being, though, she would simply have to shelve her misgivings because Josh obviously needed her tonight…and he was too young to understand the turmoil that was going on in her mind. He'd bonded with her in such a loving way that she knew she could never forget him, whatever happened in the future.

'I'd love to spend the evening with you, Josh,' she said, calmly avoiding Dan's eyes. This wasn't for Dan's sake, this was for Josh—and for her own pleasure.

Josh climbed down from Dan's lap and went across to sit on Anita's.

The swing door opened again and Rachel swept through. All eyes from the other medical professionals were on the sophisticated woman and there was a lot of whispering going on. Anita caught snippets of the hushed tones and was able to piece together what they were saying.

'A famous professor from America who's going to give the guest lectures at the university next week.'

'Yes…she's some kind of relative of Dan Mackintosh.'

'Rumour has it that she's the mother of his child.'

'That's a bit unlikely…I reckon it's more likely that Dr Anita is his mother.'

'Well, the boy certainly seems happier with her than the other woman.'

Unaware of the speculation going on around her, Rachel took a paper napkin from the container in the middle of the table and carefully wiped a plastic chair before sitting down next to Dan.

'I've enjoyed looking around your hospital, Dan. Be an angel and get me a coffee, will you? Decaf, if they have it. And how have you been, Josh? Have you been good for Anita?'

'Anita's coming to look after me tonight.'

Rachel's eyes flickered. 'That's very kind of you, Anita. But, then, you're very good with Josh. He's certainly taken to you—Oh, thank you, Dan.' She took a sip of her coffee and pulled a face. 'I do miss American coffee but that's one thing you have to put up with when you're away from home. Don't you miss living in England, Anita?'

'Not really. I was born in Rangalore so this is home to me.'

'Really! So how long do you intend to stay out here?'

'I haven't decided yet.'

'But you're on a one-year contract, Anita,' Dan put in smoothly. 'So you'll have to stay for a year at least.'

'That will depend on…on… Let's change the subject,' Anita said amiably. 'We don't need to discuss my contractual obligations now.'

'You're not thinking of leaving, are you?' Rachel said.

'For the moment, I'm happily getting on with my job.' Anita said, as she pushed back her chair and stood up. 'So, I'd better leave you all here and go back to A and E.'

Josh was already on his feet, his little hand searching for Anita's.

Dan stood up and took hold of Josh's hand. 'Stay here with Rachel and me, Josh. Anita has to get back to her work.'

'But I want to—'

'Anita will see you this evening when she comes off duty,' Rachel said. 'Come and sit beside me, Josh, and tell me everything you've seen in the hospital this afternoon. Where did Anita take you when…?'

Anita hurried out through the swing doors, happy to be going back to A and E where she knew exactly what she had to do. She would immerse herself in her work and would have no time to worry about poor little Josh struggling to get on with his mother.

A patient with gastric problems was waiting to see her, Sister explained as soon as she arrived. She took the woman into one of the examination cubicles and tried to get a clear picture of her history.

She learned that the woman was a native of New Delhi and spoke excellent English. Fifty-seven years old, she had lived in Rangalore for five years, where her husband was an executive with one of the big computer companies now based here. For the last couple of months she'd occasionally had problems swallowing.

'Not all the time, you understand, Doctor. Sometimes I can go for days without any problem and then, completely out of the blue, I'll be having a drink of water and it will bounce straight back up into my mouth.'

'Can you feel how far down your food pipe the water seems to get before it bounces back, Shahana?'

The patient leaned back against the pillows on the examination table and put her hand to the top of her chest.

'It seems to stop about here. And then… whoosh! It's back in my mouth again. I've also vomited quite unexpectedly when I haven't felt nauseous at all. It can be embarrassing if it comes on quickly and I get no warning.'

Alarm bells were ringing in Anita's mind. It sounded as if there was some kind of obstruction in the oesophagus and she knew that this kind of symptom had to be taken very seriously.

'I think I'd better take a look at what's going on in your throat. The best way would be for me to perform a gastroscopy on you, Shahana.'

'What's that?'

'I'll put a tube with a tiny camera down your throat into the oesophagus, your food pipe, and we'll be able to see on screen why you're having this problem.'

Shahana pulled a face. 'Will it hurt?'

'It's a little uncomfortable, but we'll have your throat sprayed with some local anaesthetic and that will numb the discomfort. When was the last time you had anything to eat?'

'I had a little rice with some lentils at about seven this morning and that's all.'

'That's fine! I'll see if I can organise a theatre for your gastroscopy this afternoon.'

'A gastroscopy this afternoon?' Dan said, coming into the cubicle. 'No problem. Theatre three is empty and nothing is scheduled there until tomorrow. Would you like me to give you a hand?'

Anita agreed as she took Dan across to meet her patient. Dan listened to Anita's explanation of the symptoms before doing a brief examination and answering Shahana's further questions about the procedure they were going to do. After settling their patient in a comfortable position, he drew Anita to one side, telling her he needed to discuss something with her.

Anita spoke to the nurse who was assisting

her, delegating the task of preparing her patient for Theatre before following Dan outside.

He took her into the next cubicle and waited until they were both sitting down before speaking.

'Are you thinking about leaving us?' he asked, his voice sharp with anxiety. 'Please, say you're not.'

'Dan, I don't want to talk about it now.'

He leaned forward and, placing one hand at the back of her head, drew her towards him. His eyes locked with hers.

'And I do want to talk about it,' he said firmly. 'I thought you were happy here.'

'I was…until…'

'Until Rachel arrived.' He finished her sentence for her, removing his hand and leaning back in his chair. 'Anita, Rachel is only here for a couple of weeks and then she'll be gone.'

'But will she? How can things ever be the same again now that she's met her son? She may well decide to stay on longer. She obviously adores him and she'll be making plans to see more of him. She's his mother! If I were in her shoes…'

'Yes?' he breathed, letting the question hang in the air. 'If you were Josh's mother, what would you do?'

'Well, I'm not Josh's mother so…it's all pure speculation, but it's Rachel's right to spend more time with her son, having missed so much of his childhood already.'

'Yes, of course.'

'Dr Dan.' A young nurse had come into the cubicle. 'Sorry to interrupt you, sir, but Sister would like to know if it's you or Dr Anita who is going to perform the gastroscopy.'

'We'll work together on this one, Nurse,' Dan said, standing up. 'We're on our way to Theatre now.'

'I'd like you to accompany Shahana to Theatre, Nurse,' Anita said. 'As soon as we've arranged for an anaesthetist to do the local anesthetic, we'll scrub up and get started.'

By the time they were standing either side of the theatre table all thoughts about Josh and Rachel had vanished from Anita's mind. She'd had time to ask where Josh and Rachel were while she and Dan had been scrubbing up in the ante-theatre. His answer was abrupt and to the point.

'They've gone home.'

She knew when she glanced sideways and saw his serious expression that she mustn't reopen their earlier discussion. All their concentration was now needed for the gastroscopy.

Dan elected to begin placing the gastroscope into their patient's mouth while Anita gently explained what was happening, encouraging Shahana to relax as much as she could.

'The more you relax the easier it will be for the tube to go down your gullet… Yes, that's good… Take another deep breath…nice and calm…'

Anita glanced up at the screen in front of them. Dan was having difficulty inserting the tube any further and was having to maneuver it carefully around a piece of hard tissue that shouldn't have been there if the oesophagus was healthy. She looked across the table at Dan, knowing that he had come to the same conclusion that she had. The protuberance from the wall of the oesophagus was a tumour and from the distinctive shape and colour outlined on the screen, it was almost certainly malignant.

'We need some biopsies,' Anita said quietly.

Dan nodded in agreement as Anita began to take tiny snippets of tissue from the tumour and the surrounding area. She told one of the theatre nurses to ensure that the sections of tissue were sent to the path lab as soon as possible.

Shahana was making noises in her throat, indicating that she was uncomfortable.

'Almost finished, Shahana,' Anita said, as she leaned over her patient. 'You've been great. We'll soon have you out of here.'

When the procedure was over, she accompanied her patient into the recovery room and sat down on a chair beside the bed.

'My throat feels sore, Doctor,' Shahana said croakily.

Anita put her hand on Shahana's. 'It will feel sore for a while now that the local anaesthetic is wearing off. In about an hour when all the effects of the anaesthetic have gone you'll be able to have a cup of tea. Now, you told me earlier that your husband couldn't come in with you today.'

'Yes, he's gone back to New Delhi for a few days on business. Actually, I didn't tell him I was coming to the hospital. He's always said I was making a fuss when I told him about my swallowing problem. He said it's just a bit of indigestion…which it is, isn't it?'

Anita hesitated. 'Well, I think it's something that will need further investigation. I sent some samples of the tissue around the area that's giving you the swallowing problem to our laboratory. I should get a report in the morning. Meanwhile, I think it would be a good idea if you stayed in the hospital overnight so we can discuss the findings with you tomorrow. Is there anyone else at home you should notify?'

Shahana said she would be alone if she went back so she'd like to stay.

'Good, that's settled, then. I had a word with Dr Mackintosh at the end of your gastroscopy and he agreed with me that it would be best for you to spend the night here.'

She felt a surge of relief as Dan came into the recovery room.

'I've organised a room for Shahana. A nurse and a porter will take you there, Shahana.'

As soon as their patient had been wheeled out of Recovery, Dan suggested they should both go along to his office.

'To continue our discussion,' he said evenly.

They walked side by side along the corridor, Anita ensuring that her fingers were in no danger of contacting Dan's. She wanted to remain totally dispassionate about the situation they found themselves in and also she didn't want the prying eyes of the other medical staff to augment the various rumours that were being tossed around on the grapevine.

Sunita, Dan's secretary, brought in coffee as soon as they arrived. She put a couple of letters on his desk for his signature before retiring discreetly to her room.

'You asked for the biopsy report to be ready in the morning, didn't you, Anita?'

'Of course…although from the visual aspect
I'd say it's almost certainly malignant.'

He breathed out. 'It certainly does look as if
we've got an oesophageal tumour there. Such
bad luck! How old is Shahana?'

'Fifty-seven. We'll start chemotherapy and ra-
diotherapy to shrink the tumour as soon as we
can. Then, hopefully, she can have surgery to
remove it. What do you think, Dan?'

'It's a difficult operation. I think we should get
all the tests done before we look that far ahead.
If she's a suitable candidate for surgery and the
cancer is contained in that one area of the body,
we can operate.'

She leaned back in her chair and took a sip of
coffee. 'So many ifs and buts in the medical pro-
fession. We're at the mercy of so many things
that might happen before surgery is possible. I
think I've had enough problems for the day. Tell
me what's happening this evening.'

'I'll drive you back home with me when we've
finished our coffee,' Dan said. 'Rachel and Josh
will already be there, of course, and I expect

Samaya will have given Josh an early supper. I phoned her before we did the gastroscopy to tell her you will be there to put Josh to bed. She's planning to give you supper afterwards.'

'Samaya is wonderful!'

'But it's good of you to come out to be with Josh, Anita. Samaya would have put him to bed but it means so much to him to have you there with him.'

'What time will you be back from your dinner with Rachel?'

He hesitated. 'I'm not sure. I've arranged for my usual taxi firm to collect you at eleven tonight to bring you back to the hospital. Rachel and I will be very late, I imagine?'

A cold hand seemed to be clutching at her heart as she listened to him speaking. *Rachel and I will be very late.* Josh's parents going out to dinner together...as a couple. What a charming couple they would make. Meanwhile, she would take care of Josh and then go home. She didn't know what to make of it all.

'So Rachel is staying the night with you?' she said as calmly as she could. She wasn't going to stoop to raise her voice. She just had to know where she stood.

'It's going to be after midnight. She'll stay in the guest suite. She wants to have a discussion about Josh's future tonight just as soon as we can reasonably escape from the dinner.'

'After midnight?'

'Well, it will have to be after the dinner so, yes, it will be after midnight,' Dan said defensively.

'How cosy! Just the two of you discussing your son's future…at home before you both go to bed and—'

'Rachel will be sleeping in the guest suite.'

'Of course she will!' Anita put down her cup and stood up. 'I'd like to go to your house now to be with Josh.'

Josh was one person she could trust.

CHAPTER NINE

ANITA lay awake for long periods during the night. After the taxi had dropped her off at the hospital, she'd made a determined effort to switch off all thoughts of what might be happening between Rachel and Dan but it was impossible.

She'd tried to enjoy her evening with Josh after Rachel and Dan had departed to their dinner with the vice chancellor. Outwardly, she was sure that she'd hadn't shown the sadness she had felt when she'd sat beside the bath, chatting to Josh, occasionally pushing one of his boats up and down the water, engineering a race between her boat and Josh's. Certainly, he'd laughed with excitement and gone to sleep exhausted but happy after she'd read him a story.

But as soon as she'd gone downstairs to her

supper, which Samaya had set in the dining room, she'd felt a cold loneliness enveloping her. Samaya had excused herself and gone to her room, saying that she would listen for Josh after Anita had gone back to the hospital.

She had pushed the cold meat and salad around her plate, taken a tiny bite, chewed, agreed with herself it was delicious but had put her fork down at the side of her plate. The platter of tropical fruits had been easy to digest. She'd taken her plates to the kitchen and gone into the small room where Dan kept most of his books. Apart from the medical books, which made up the majority, he had a number of novels, crime, detective stories, adventure, the usual masculine stuff. So he obviously hadn't had a resident woman in his life. Or if he had, she'd removed all her traces—or she hadn't stayed long enough to make an impact.

There was a short section on travel. That would while away the time until the taxi arrived. There was a book on the beaches of Goa. Her parents had sometimes taken her there when she'd been a small child, she remembered. How wonderful it would be to travel back there with Dan and Josh.

She leaned back in the armchair, telling herself that was pure fantasy. None of this fairy-tale stuff was going to happen to her now that Rachel had come back to see her son.

It was a relief when she heard the taxi pulling into the drive. She closed the book and got her things, carefully closing the front door so that it locked.

But now, lying in her bed in the doctors' quarters of the hospital, it was impossible to rid herself of the negative thoughts she'd been pushing away all evening. Rachel was back in Dan's life for good, and even though Josh didn't like her yet, it was inevitable that at some point they would bond. And the family would be a complete unit.

There seemed no permanent place for her in Dan's life. It was too full already. It would break her heart, again but she'd better start making plans for the future.

For the next few days Anita threw all her energies into her work at the hospital, deliberately avoiding discussions about Rachel with Dan. She confined herself to discussions about patients.

They went together to see Shahana to break the news as gently as possible that the biopsies of the tumour in her oesophagus had shown that it was malignant. They outlined the treatment that she would undergo, arranged for her husband to return early from his business trip to be with her and gave her all the support she needed.

Shahana took the news calmly and proved to be a strong patient, determined to beat the cancer she was facing. Anita made a point of calling in to see her every day even though her patient had been handed over to the cancer unit.

'It's so good of you to take so much trouble with me, Doctor,' Shahana said one evening when Anita called in at the end of a long, busy day. 'You must be longing to get off duty, aren't you?'

Anita sat down on the chair at the bedside. 'Yes, but I wanted to make sure you were OK.'

'It means a lot to me that you call in like this for a chat. Chanu, my husband, is busy with his work and I haven't got a lot of friends down here in Rangalore—all my close friends and relatives live in the north of India. I do miss them at a time like this. Don't you sometimes wish you were back in the UK, Doctor?'

'Do call me Anita. I'm very happy working here. I was born in Rangalore and my father was a doctor at the old hospital here.'

'Really? How fascinating. What was it like as a child here?'

'I loved it!' Anita regaled her patient with stories of coming to see her father working in the hospital and playing at home with her small school friends.

'Where is the house you lived in, Anita?' Shahana asked when Anita had been speaking for a few minutes.

Anita smiled. 'It was very close to the hospital but it was pulled down a few years ago to make way for extensions to this new hospital we're in. Some of the garden still remains at the back of the hospital here. There's an old eucalyptus tree where my father fixed a swing for me. I sometimes go and look at it—touch the bark, remember those long-ago days…'

'Is the swing still there?'

'No. It was an affair my father concocted one evening, I remember. The rope will have perished a long time ago.'

She hadn't noticed that Dan had arrived on the ward and was making his way to Shahana's bed.

'Oh, Dr Mackintosh, has Anita told you about her childhood here in Rangalore? It's absolutely fascinating. It's really taken my mind off my problems tonight.'

'I've heard some of the stories,' Dan said. 'And I'm glad it's made you feel better, Shahana. I've come to remind Anita she should have gone off duty.'

'I'm off duty now,' Anita said, standing up. 'I'll see you tomorrow, Shahana.'

Dan walked beside her down the ward. As they went out into the corridor he said, 'It's good of you to spend time with Shahana and it's obviously therapeutic for her.'

'It's therapeutic for me as well. When I'm with

Shahana watching the way she's facing her cancer, it reminds me that my own problems are unimportant.'

'I take it you're talking about us and the situation with Rachel?'

She continued walking along the corridor in the direction of the doctors' quarters but she didn't reply. She didn't want to start the argument again.

Dan put a hand on her arm and drew her to a halt. 'We have to talk.'

'We've talked enough. I'm seeing how things develop before…before…'

'Before what, Anita?'

'Before I decide whether to stay on here or…or leave.'

'Anita, I don't want you to go, you're under a contractual obligation. You can't—'

'Oh, but I can if I have to.'

'Come home with me tonight. Please, Anita.'

'Will Rachel be there?'

He hesitated. 'I don't know. She's trying to spend as much time as she can with Josh so she sometimes stays over…in the guest suite. But, Anita, nothing is going on between us! She's my ex-wife, visiting her son, trying to form a bond with him after missing his early childhood. Our relationship was over years ago when Josh was a baby and we saw that our marriage was in tatters. You have to believe me. It's only for the sake of bonding with her son that she stays over occasionally, so she can see him at breakfast, that kind of thing.'

Anita swallowed hard as she wished fervently that she could believe him, that she could banish the awful jealousy that was threatening to take over her life.

'Dan, I'm tired. I'm going to my room for a shower and an early night so I'll see you tomorrow.'

As she walked hurriedly away she was aware that he was still watching her. But he hadn't tried to dissuade her.

Anita went down to A and E very early next morning. It was easier to get up and start working than toss and turn in her bed, while her mind went over and over the possibilities of how she was going to handle her relationship with Dan. She had an overwhelming feeling that her brief interlude of a second chance with him was coming to a close.

The night staff were still on duty. Night Sister looked up from her desk at the nurses' station and smiled.

'Didn't expect to see you so early, Anita. Couldn't you sleep?'

Anita gave her a wry grin. 'Well, funny you should say that.'

'That makes two of you!'

'What do you mean?'

'Dan is in his office. He arrived a couple of hours ago, saying he had work to catch up on. But I didn't believe him. What's going on between you two?'

'I don't know what you mean.'

'Well, Dan asked if you'd go to see him as soon as you arrived. I'm just passing on his message, that's all, so don't look at me like that!'

'Thanks. I'll check out what he wants, then.'

Anita turned away, aware that Sister Fenisha was grinning from ear to ear. And two of her junior nurses, who had been listening in, were whispering together. She had no idea what her colleagues were making of her relationship with Dan but she was sure they were providing lots of juicy rumours for their own entertainment.

It was strangely quiet as she walked along the corridor to Dan's office. She felt an overwhelming sense of foreboding as she tapped on his door.

'Anita, I didn't expect you so early! Come in, come in.' He held the door wide open.

She remained very still and calm as she looked up at him. 'Sister said you wanted to see me.'

'I've made some coffee. Sunita hasn't arrived yet so we won't be overheard.'

He sounded as nervous as she felt. He motioned to her to go over to the seating area near the window and placed a cup of coffee on the occasional table between two armchairs.

'We need to clear the air.' His eyes locked with hers.

She took a sip of coffee. 'You mean about Rachel?'

'About us.'

'Dan, all those years ago when you told me we had to end our relationship, while I understand why it happened, I was devastated and with Rachel back on the scene—well, I don't trust the situation. I couldn't bear to have my heart broken again.'

He leaned forward. 'It was the hardest thing I'd ever had to do in my life—say goodbye to the woman I loved.' He put down his coffee-cup on the small table in front of them. 'The three months we lived together were was the most idyllic I've ever had. I was madly in love with you. I wanted to marry you and have a family with you, stay together for the rest of our lives. I hoped you would feel the same way but I couldn't discuss it with you until I knew what chance I had of fulfilling that dream.'

She remained silent as she watched him struggling to find the right words.

'The day before you started to tell me how

much you wanted a family I'd been told for the final time there was absolutely no possibility I could father a child.'

'So my timing wasn't very good, was it?' she said.

He took a deep breath. 'I was devastated. I could see how passionately you felt about having your own family.' His eyes locked with hers. 'I knew I had to tell you it wasn't possible with me…and I knew I had to let you go, to follow your own dream…without me. And after our discussion I also knew that I would have to be the one to make the break. Because I knew you would cling to the hope of a miracle happening. You do see that I did it for your sake, don't you?'

'Yes,' she said carefully. 'But it hurt so much not to be able to discuss it further with you.'

He put an arm around her shoulders and drew her against him. 'I'm sorry. Maybe I was wrong. I thought a clean break at that point would be easier on you, that it would save you greater pain in the long run. I just wanted you to find the kind of life I thought I couldn't give you.'

'And then the miracle happened—you were made fertile again,' she breathed.

He swallowed hard. 'I was ecstatic when the specialist in America gave me the good news.' He paused. 'But by then it was too late for you and me to be together.'

'Yes,' she said quietly.

He relaxed his grip on her shoulders. 'It was similar to a bereavement when I found out that you were marrying another man. The sense of loss I felt was…'

He choked and Anita took hold of his hand, looking up into his eyes, which were moist with tears.

'When Bella died I thought I would never love again but then you came along and my new life began.'

'What happened on the day she died?' Anita asked gently.

He leaned back against the cushions of the seating area. 'We'd had breakfast together. I'd gone to the hospital. She'd gone for her hair appointment. There were stairs to climb up to the salon. One of the assistants saw her stumble on the steps and fall backwards to the foot of the staircase. An ambulance was called but she couldn't be revived. At the inquest the coroner concluded that the aneurism had finally burst.'

'I can't imagine how you must have felt to lose the woman you—'

'Anita, let's not waste any more time!' He stood up, drawing her to her feet so that he could entwine her in his arms. 'Life is so…so…unpredictable. You and I were made for each other.'

He bent his head and kissed her, very gently at first and then with a deep passion that threatened to overwhelm them both with its intensity. In any other situation he knew he would have swept her off her feet and carried her off somewhere where they could make love.

He raised his head and looked down at her. She gazed back at him, feeling desperately sorry for all he'd suffered but at the same time a little voice was telling her not to get swept away on a sea of compassion.

'When Rachel goes back to America—' she began, but he cut her short.

'Ah…there's a small problem there.'

She moved in his arms as she felt him tense up. As he released his hold on her she walked over to the window, staring out across the garden to the old eucalyptus tree where her childhood swing had been.

'What kind of problem?' she asked.

'There's a possibility she may be staying on to work at the university, possibly joining one of the surgical firms here at the hospital. It's early days and nothing has been finalised but she's had offers of work. I know she wants to spend more time with Josh so if she were here in Rangalore, that would make things easier for her.'

He put his arm around her again, placing his hands gently on her shoulders. His touch was very comforting but it did nothing to sort out the emotional turmoil going on inside her.

Anita swung round. 'So where would she live?'

'We haven't got as far as discussing that yet. For the moment she's happy to come and go when she pleases and spend the occasional night in the guest suite.'

Anita drew in a breath so she couldn't say something she might regret.

But Dan could read her face. 'Rachel has told me she'd like to spend Saturday and Sunday looking after Josh,' he said. 'She's requested that Samaya be there to help her but I think she wants to experience what it's like to be a real mother. She's here for Josh, not me.'

He put his finger under her chin and raised it so that she had to look directly into his eyes.

'So, I've got a plan. I shall be, theoretically, not be needed this weekend so would you come away with me on Saturday? We'll come back on Sunday and...'

'But is that fair on Josh?'

'She is his mother!'

Don't remind me! 'Yes, but she doesn't seem to have much maternal instinct.'

'It will come. She just needs practice. And Samaya will be there so nothing can happen that will hurt Josh in any way.' He took a deep breath.

'Anita, I really want to take you away from all this… Give ourselves a chance. We'll fly to Goa—it's only an hour by plane. I know a place near to Paradise Beach where—'

'Paradise Beach? Is that really its name?'

'Paradise Beach is what everybody who's ever been there call it. The bay we'll stay at is nearby. It's much quieter, unknown to the extent that you can hear nothing but the waves lapping on the shore at night. I took Josh there once and he loved it. But this time it's just the two of us. What do you say?'

What could she say? Could she put her doubts and fears on hold for a whole weekend and simply live for each precious moment?

'Dan, it sounds idyllic but if—'

'No ifs or buts! Just say you'll come.'

'Yes, all right. I'd love to!'

As soon as she'd spoken she felt as if a weight had been lifted off her shoulders. She was going to spend a whole weekend with Dan and she wasn't going to spoil it by thinking about the past or the future. The two days together would be all that concerned her. A chance to find out what they really had together.

He held her close for a moment, before releasing her. 'I'll get on the phone and book the flights and the cabin near the beach.'

'So we'll be staying in a cabin?'

'Thatched roof, like a shack, but wait till you see the view from the veranda! Completely out of this world.' He turned away and went across to his desk. 'I'd better phone now because the particular one I want is much sought after.'

'I'll go and start work.'

He was already punching in the digits on his phone as she left him.

For the rest of the day they met only briefly but Anita felt much calmer now that she'd made the decision to go away with Dan for the weekend. After she returned she would assess the situation, but for the moment she was feeling happier than she had since she'd arrived back in Rangalore.

They came together in the middle of the afternoon when Anita called in Dan for a second opinion on a patient.

A woman of twenty, newly married, had been brought in with intense abdominal pain. Anita, feeling the tender area to the right of the patient's groin knew that this could be a classic case of appendicitis or it could be a case of an embryo developing in a Fallopian tube. While she was waiting for Dan to turn up she did all the usual tests and sent blood samples off for urgent analysis at the laboratory.

By the time Dan arrived from Theatre she had taken her patient to one of the emergency units.

He came in, still in theatre greens, his mask hanging down. 'I can fit this patient in next on my list,' he said quietly. 'It sounded urgent when you phoned me. Whichever diagnosis is correct, we need to operate as soon as possible. I'm short of an assistant for the next hour so if you could come along and scrub up, that would help.'

'Yes, I'll just let Sister Razia know where I'll be.'

Dan glanced at the test results. 'High temperature is indicative of both situations. Ah, positive pregnancy result…I'll just take a look.'

'I think it's ectopic,' Anita said. 'Look at this result here.'

Dan nodded in agreement as he moved over to the patient and began his examination. He was even more convinced afterwards as he explained to the patient about the impending operation.

'I'll see you up in Theatre in…as soon as you can make it.'

He hurried out of the room, almost colliding with the porter that Anita had ordered.

'Give me a couple of minutes,' she said to the porter. 'I've just got to finish off the pre-ops and then we can be on our way.'

She faced Dan across the operating table, passing him the scalpel he'd requested with her sterile gloved hand.

He made a small incision low down in the abdomen and began his exploration of the affected tissues. Anita leaned forward, anxious to have her own diagnosis confirmed by the physical evidence in front of her.

'We've certainly got an ectopic pregnancy in this Fallopian tube,' Dan said. 'I can't save the tube. It's too badly damaged. I'll have to excise it.'

He fell silent as he concentrated on his work. Anita felt the usual disappointment that part of the reproductive organs of a patient were going to be taken away, but she agreed with Dan that there was no alternative.

Talking earlier to Hasina, her patient, she'd learned that the young woman was desperate to start a family. Taking away one Fallopian tube meant that her chances of becoming pregnant were reduced, but she'd known patients like this who had gone on to conceive later. They would just have to hope. She made a mental note to call in and tell her patient this later on in the day when she came round from the anaesthetic.

She sutured the internal tissues and the edges of the incision after Dan had removed the Fallopian tube. It would be a neat scar and should fade with the passing of time.

'Thanks, Anita,' Dan said, as he peeled off his mask and tossed it into the bin. 'I've got an assistant arriving soon for the rest of the morning so you can go back to A and E now.'

'Thank you, Sir.' She smiled at him as she went out through the swing doors, thinking how much easier her rapport with Dan had become since their talk that morning. Now all they had to do was keep it like this when they were away in Goa at the weekend. She hugged her excitement deep down inside her.

CHAPTER TEN

'IT'S absolutely idyllic!'

Anita stood still so that she could appreciate the beauty of the wooden, thatched-roofed cabin they were approaching. It had been a steep climb up the cliff path to reach it but the effort had been worth it. She breathed in deeply so that she would stop panting and looked out across the sea.

'My parents brought me to Goa a couple of times when I was small. But it was further up the coast. I don't know this area at all.'

'I know, but remembering it from the time I was here with Josh, I knew it was the place I wanted to bring you.'

'How did you keep him from the edge of the cliff?'

'With difficulty! It was last year. I never let him

out of my sight—but he's a sensible boy and recognises danger when I stress the importance of staying close beside me. Come and have a look inside.'

The interior was exquisitely rustic. Wooden armchairs in the tiny sitting room were made comfortable by cotton throws and cushions. Behind this area there was a small bedroom with a small double bed. As it was already early evening someone had covered the bed with a mosquito net. And behind that a door led to a tiny shower cubicle. Buckets of water with lids on were standing by to be poured into the cistern above the shower head.

'Very rustic,' Dan grinned. 'And if you're wondering where the loo is, you have to go out of the door at the front and walk round the back to a tiny hut where there's a contrivance that serves the purpose—very green and healthy for the planet, that sort of thing.'

'Well, pipes fixed to the hillside would have been rather unsightly, wouldn't they, even if it was possible. I think it's amazing they could have made it so comfortable on the top of this cliff.'

'A bit of basic living is worth it for the view…and the wonder of spending a whole weekend alone with you with no work to be done and nobody to please but ourselves.'

Anita's heart was too full to reply. A whole weekend alone together, away from all their tensions.

Dan dumped his travel bag on the floor and turned to take her in his arms. She barely had time to drop her own bag on the floor before she found herself swept up in a tide of mutual passion.

Their passion had started simmering on the small plane that had brought them to the nearby field that served as an airfield. As soon as she'd felt Dan's thigh touching hers in the cramped seats she'd wanted him. They'd quite unashamedly flirted with each other like a couple of teenagers for the whole journey. They'd talked together in hushed whispers, their eyes communicating what they were both agreeing on…what they knew would happen as soon as they were alone.

At last here they were in their own little cosy nest on the clifftop like a couple of lovebirds. She found herself tearing at his clothes, longing to feel skin on skin. They both crawled under the mosquito net, laughing as they tried not to become entangled. But it caused a short period of frustration before they could settle down and make love.

All part of the fun, Anita thought as she felt Dan's hands caressing her body. Mmm…this was what she had been waiting for, longing for… To be in his arms again was a dream come true…

It was dark when Anita woke up. She had memories of feeling utterly delirious with sexual excitement before she'd fallen asleep. She remembered calling out Dan's name over and over again as they'd made love until she'd felt she couldn't climax any more…and then she had, again and again and again…until she'd floated away on a cloud, way out to sea, into the oblivion where nothing mattered any more except the love you felt for the one person in the world who was meant for you…

Dan raised his head from the pillow beside her. In the moonlight streaming through the tiny window she could make out his handsome face. She reached across and traced the side of his cheek with her finger.

'I love you, Anita,' he said huskily.

He lowered his head and kissed her gently. He drew her against him, oh, so close, and kissed her more deeply. She felt her body melting again, moulding itself against his until the urgency of their coupling took over and they became one body striving for the same purpose of giving the ultimate in pleasure to each other.

Later, they padded naked out to the tiny veranda with its insect repellent mesh sides and sat down on the wooden bench seat, arranging the cushions to make it more comfortable. Anita lay back against Dan, his arms clasped around her breasts, as they looked out across the moonlit water.

'It's so beautiful, Dan, as if we've escaped the world and found our own little piece of heaven.'

He drew her closer against his muscular chest. 'We have escaped the world, Anita…for a short time anyway…'

She wouldn't allow thoughts of returning to reality to cloud her blissful weekend.

'Yes, it really is heaven up here,' she breathed. 'Listen…there's no sound except the sound of the sea.'

The blissful silence continued, each making sure that thoughts of the world beyond stayed that way, way beyond their consciousness here in their own special hideaway.

'Are you hungry?' Dan asked, after a while.

'I was when we arrived, but now…'

'I'll make supper-breakfast,' Dan said, easing her out of his arms and standing up.

'Is there food here?'

'Is there food?' he joked. 'Just you hold on, madam. Stay right where you are so that I can wait on you.'

There was a tiny bottled gas stove in the corner of the sitting room and above it a mesh cage hanging from the ceiling to protect the food inside from insects. Reaching inside the cage, Dan produced bacon, eggs and a chunky loaf of bread.

She laughed as he tied a blue and white striped butcher's apron around his naked body.

'Is that to keep your skin clean, Dan?'

'Well, cooking bacon is a very dangerous operation. A man could do himself a great deal of damage if he didn't gown up correctly. Now, where do they keep the scalpels and spatulas in this establishment?'

She realised that she was actually ravenous when Dan placed their meal on a tiny wooden table in front of them. As she finished her bacon and eggs, wiping up the delicious yolk with a piece of the crusty bread, she felt she had never been happier. Here, with Dan, she was totally at peace with the world and nothing could possibly destroy this feeling, this moment.

Looking out towards the horizon, she could see the first pink flush of dawn over the surface of the sea.

'We saw the sunset through the bedroom window in between...' He nuzzled his head against her neck. 'Do you remember?'

She nodded, knowing that was the most wonderful sunset she'd ever seen. The whole experience had been magic. Making love while the sun disappeared in a fiery glow.

'Now we're going to see the sun rise,' Dan said huskily, putting his arm around her and drawing her against him.

They watched as the wonder of the sunrise began to unfold. First a tiny spot of red light appeared to come up out of the sea then, at first slowly and then very quickly, came the round crimson ball. As it emerged it seemed to send hot red flames darting out over the water.

Anita shielded her eyes. 'It's so beautiful.'

Then a cold chill ran through her but she told herself that the idyllic rapport that now existed between them could, somehow last for ever.

As if her premonition of a change for the worse had been correct, she heard the shrilling of a mobile phone.

Dan frowned as he removed his arm from Anita's shoulders. 'I asked only to be contacted if there was an emergency with Josh.'

He hurried through to the bedroom, searching

through the pile of clothes they'd tossed on the floor.

'Oh, Josh, it's you. Are you OK?'

Dan returned to the veranda, his phone clamped to his ear, and sat down on the bench. As Anita listened she gathered that Josh had persuaded Rachel to let him phone Dan because he'd woken up early and couldn't get back to sleep. Then Rachel came on the phone and Dan checked that there was no real emergency.

'Well, yes, of course we won't be late, Rachel. How are you coping? Excellent! Well, you both seem to be enjoying yourselves…apart from the early morning wake-up call.' Dan laughed at something that Rachel had said. 'Well, that's what parenting is all about, isn't it? I thought I'd throw you in at the deep end and make you swim. And it seems to have worked.'

He was listening again to the sound of an excited Rachel. Again he laughed at something she'd said. Anita got up and went into the bedroom. There was a definite early morning chill in the air which she hadn't noticed before.

Dan, chatting on the phone with the mother of his child, sounded just like a normal father talking to his wife. And the rapport between Josh and his mother seemed to have improved.

She pulled on her sandals and tied a sarong around her then walked out through the veranda where Dan was still on the phone, leaning back easily against the wall, enjoying hearing the exploits of his family. He didn't seem to notice she'd gone as she walked along the side of the veranda and made her way to the toilet on the rocky slope at the back of the cabin.

Dan was still on the phone when she returned, padding her way barefoot through to the bedroom again.

The bucket of water suspended above the shower responded to her tug on the rope and a cascade of tepid water ran down her body. Mmm, that felt good!

'Hang on, I'll come and fix a second bucket full for you, Anita! Rachel, I've got to go… Yes, see you tonight.'

Anita wished she hadn't heard that last

sentence as she rubbed herself vigorously with soap, but he'd told her he loved her, she had to hang on to that.

Dan came in, looking both relieved and apologetic. 'I'm sorry for the interruption, Anita. But fortunately everything's fine at home,' he said as he fixed a second bucket over the shower.

He stepped into the shower beside her. 'Two can shower as easily as one,' he said, as he pulled the rope that released the soothing cascade.

The closeness of their bodies meant inevitably that they both wanted to go back to the rumpled bed. Anita, roused once more, put all thoughts of return to reality on hold…

Later they swam then lay close together on the warm sand until they were dry enough to put on shorts and T-shirts and walk round the corner to a shack which Dan said served excellent fresh seafood.

They sat under the fan, looking out to sea, watching the dolphins while they waited for their lunch to be cooked.

First they shared a bowl of charcoal-grilled tiger prawns, squeezing the limes which they had watched the young waiter pluck from a tree at the edge of the beach. Next they were presented with a magnificent kingfish, artistically garnished with slices of tomato placed on its silver-scaled side.

Dan picked up the large knife with an exaggerated surgical flourish and slit the fish's backbone expertly, turning both sides outwards to reveal the succulent creamy flesh.

The fish was delicious. A large bowl of oranges, bananas, grapes and papaya appeared at the end of the meal.

Dan reached across the table and fed her a grape. She chewed slowly before swallowing, her eyes still locked on Dan's.

He glanced down briefly at his watch. 'Time to go,' he said quietly.

'Yes.'

'In fact, we ought to go right now.'

'I'm ready.'

'I'll pay the bill.'

They were lingering, clinging to their precious

time. They held hands as they made their way back to the cabin where they'd left their luggage. Anita shrugged into her jeans and long-sleeved shirt. Dan was already dressed in chinos and a clean shirt and was paying the boy who'd guarded the cabin for them during the morning.

By that evening they would be back in civilization with all it would entail. She smiled at Dan as she stepped outside into the bright sunlight.

'Let's go!'

Dan dropped her off at the hospital. She'd insisted she wasn't going to go back home with him to his home.

'Let Rachel finish off her weekend in charge of Josh,' she said firmly.

'She seems to be doing OK,' he said. 'But, yes, you're right.'

'OK! I'll see you in the morning.'

He leapt out to open the car door for her. Bending his head, he kissed her gently on the cheek. Far too many prying eyes for lip contact! Their taxi driver had already carried her bag to the front entrance of the hospital where a porter was waiting to carry it up to her room.

Minutes later she was alone. She closed the door and leaned against it. The idyll was over. Now she had to come to terms with reality, with the fact that Rachel now seemed to be firmly ensconced at Dan's house. Josh had accepted her; a real family unit had been formed. And she still had no idea where she fitted into the equation.

After all these years of longing for Dan she'd finally spent the most idyllic, heavenly weekend with him. He'd told her he loved her and she believed him. Yet there still seemed so much in the way. How could she feel sure they could have a real future together, especially if Rachel stayed?

During the next two weeks the hospital grapevine was buzzing with stories about the Professor Crawford, who was wowing students and medical staff alike with her lectures at the university. Dan told Anita he'd been to a couple of them and had found them very stimulating. He said he hadn't realised how good she was in her particular field.

Anita tried not to feel jealous when he enthused about Rachel but even though it was on a professional level, it didn't help her fragile emotional state. One good thing that had emerged from the fact that Rachel was doing her two-week stint of lectures was that she was based permanently back at her hotel.

The evenings Anita spent with Dan and Josh were becoming even more precious to her now. Sometimes they went out as a threesome to a restaurant for an early supper. Other times they left Josh with Samaya and had the evening to themselves. But all the time Anita felt unsettled.

Sitting in the canteen one day, she could hear from a group of medical students at the next table what they thought about Rachel.

'She's an amazing woman…really knows her stuff…'

'And makes it interesting. I was hovering between medicine and surgery, but I'm definitely going to choose surgery now.'

'And she's easy on the eye as well!'

Loud laughter from the other students.

'I reckon you fancy her!'

Dan walked in and sat down at Anita's table.

'They're talking about Rachel,' she whispered. 'Her lectures are a great success apparently, like you told me.'

'Yes, she's certainly found her niche in life.' He pointed to her cup. 'Can I get you another coffee?'

'No, thanks. I've got to get back to A and E.'

He put out a hand to detain her. 'Don't go just yet. I just wanted to spend a few moments with you and say I won't be in the hospital tomorrow. I'm taking a day off.'

She waited for him to elaborate but he was listening in to the conversation at the next table.

'That fabulous red hair!'

Dan smiled and then leaned forward to touch Anita's face tenderly.

Anita looked down pensively. 'Has Rachel decided if she's going to take the appointment here in Rangalore?'

'I really couldn't say. I haven't seen her since the lecture I went to a couple of days ago and we didn't have time to talk afterwards.'

Anita stood up. 'Got to go!'

He stood up. 'I'll walk back to the department with you.'

'No, stay and have your coffee.'

She walked on. She'd come to a decision and
there was no point in prolonging the agony.
Rumours were circulating that Rachel had been
offered an important position at the university
which also entailed some hands-on surgery at the
hospital. Rachel's future here in Rangalore was
certainly looking rosy.

Whereas her own future was going to take a
different course to the one she'd hoped for. She
couldn't allow herself to let any emotion creep
into her decision otherwise she knew she would
go under completely—just like she'd done the
last time they'd split up.

She threw herself into her work next day,
knowing that there was no possibility that she
would see Dan at the hospital. She planned to go
and see him at home early that evening. It was
time to tell him that she wanted to be released

from her hospital contract and whatever legal steps were necessary for this to happen she would take them. She loved Dan so much, and Josh, but she couldn't live with this uncertainty any longer and she didn't want to stand in the way of any family life they might have together if Rachel stayed.

During the day she treated three survivors of a two-car collision. Miraculously their injuries weren't life-threatening. A fractured tibia of the woman passenger in one of the cars and cuts which required suturing to the two men in the other car. The fact that both cars had been travelling reasonable slowly along a country lane had helped to minimise their injuries.

She dealt with a suspected heart attack, discovering that the true diagnosis was asthma, which her middle-aged patient didn't know he had. She admitted him to a medical ward for tests and future treatment planning so that if another attack like the one he'd just suffered occurred, he would know how to handle it.

She gave one hundred per cent to her job all

day and then it was time to sort out her personal life. She felt as if she was some kind of robot as she pushed away any doubts that tried to creep into her head.

Going off duty, she hailed a cab at the front gates and gave the driver Dan's address. As they went up the drive towards the house she could feel butterflies churning in her stomach. This was the last time she would come up this drive because she wasn't going to change her mind. She'd agonised for two weeks about what she was going to do and she would stay on course however Dan reacted to her plan.

Samaya opened the front door as she approached. 'Welcome, Anita. Dan and Josh aren't here. They've been out all day, but I'm expecting them back soon.'

Another taxi was coming up the drive. Anita drew in her breath as she watched Rachel alight from the taxi, charming the driver as she gave him an obviously large amount of rupees.

'Anita! At last! I'm so glad you're here because we need to talk. Samaya, could you bring us some tea through to the veranda and turn the thermostat to very cold on the air-conditioning, please? Oh, and could you gather up those medical files I left in the library? I need to take them away with me. I've had such a long hot day! I thought I was never going to be able to get away. You know how it is, Anita, when everybody wants to talk to you just when you're trying to escape and…'

The monologue continued as Rachel headed imperiously through the house towards the veranda.

She settled herself in a chair on the veranda. Rachel chose a chair under the fan and lowered her briefcase to the wooden floor.

'Phew, what a day! Ah, thank you, Samaya. What a treasure you are!'

Samaya put the teatray down on the central table. Anita got up and poured two cups, handing one to Rachel before returning to her chair.

Rachel took a sip then placed her cup on the small table beside her. 'It's a good chance for you and I to have a heart-to-heart talk while Dan and Josh are out.'

Anita waited expectantly. 'What did you want to talk about, Rachel?'

'I just want to set a few things straight, Anita. Dan is a dear friend, a long-time friend, my ex-husband, a professional colleague, nothing more, and never will be.' She paused. 'You see, we rather rushed into our marriage. We seemed to be getting on so well and we had lots in common. I told Dan I wanted a career, but my biological clock was ticking away and I was feeling the urge to marry and have a child. I knew Dan wanted a family, too. I foolishly imagined that maternal instinct would flood through me after our baby was born but it didn't happen. The birth was awful! And after Josh was born I...'

Rachel stood up as, for once in her life, words failed her. She paced the veranda to the end and then back again, before pulling her chair closer to Anita.

Anita saw the anguish in her eyes. 'Was that when you developed postnatal depression?'

Rachel nodded. 'I couldn't cope. Josh was a sickly baby, cried a lot. I just couldn't bond with him. And I found I couldn't bond with Dan any more either. The strain really threw up the weakness in our relationship. Dan felt the same and I came to realize that he had married on the rebound and was still in love with you. He suffered feelings of guilt as a result—over our marriage, too. But he was a wonderful father to Josh. He took on all the responsibility and ensured he had a happy childhood, whereas I…'

She spread her hands wide in a gesture of despair at her own incompetence.

'How long did your postnatal depression last?'

Rachel looked sheepish. 'I would say I was probably clinically depressed for about three months. Then, when I still couldn't face motherhood, I found myself hiding in my work.'

'So why have you tried to bond at this late stage?'

'Oh, Anita, you've no idea how guilty I've felt since I opted out of my share of the responsibilities of rearing Josh! I engineered this assignment here in Rangalore so that I could try to make amends. I thought that maybe, now Josh was older, I would be able to have some sort of relationship with him. And then you were here, someone who obviously adores both him and his father someone who could so obviously be a wonderful mother to Josh..'

'You think that I want to take your place?'

'This isn't my place! It never was and never will be! Anita, if you're with Dan and Josh I will finally lose the guilt that's haunted me ever since Josh was born. I'll know that he's got a real mother to care for him.'

'But when you asked to spend a whole weekend with Josh while we were away, I thought that was because you wanted to bond with your child.'

'Your weekend away was Dan's idea! He wanted me to try to ease the tension between Josh and me. He also wanted to create a romantic weekend just for the two of you. I went along with it, and it was such hard work! I did the best job I could but I couldn't wait for Dan to get back and take over again. No, I've made the right decision today. I'm going back to the States in a couple of days. My flight's booked.'

'But I heard you were going to stay on at the university. Haven't you been offered a post there?'

Rachel nodded. 'I must admit I was tempted. But in my heart of hearts I knew it wasn't going to work out for me here. Oh, I'll stay in touch with everybody here. And I'll be a mother to the extent that I won't forget birthdays and I'll meet up with Josh if he ever asks to see me when he's older. But Josh needs you. He loves you as if you were his real mother. And Dan is so in love with you I can't imagine—'

She broke off and stared at the doorway. Dan was standing there, holding Josh's hand.

'Anita!' Josh hurled himself at her. 'I didn't know you were coming today.' He snuggled himself on her lap.

'Dan, I've just come to collect those medical files I left in your library when I was working on a lecture during that weekend you spent away with Anita,' Rachel said quickly. 'But it was so wonderful that Anita was here. I've been able to have that heart-to-heart talk I'd been planning to arrange as soon as I could find a mutually convenient time. You see, I've only got a couple of nights at the hotel and then I'm flying back to the States.'

Dan strode across the veranda and sat down in a chair next to Anita and Josh. 'Yes, the vice chancellor just phoned me and told me you'd turned down his offer.'

Rachel stood up. 'I'm sure I've made the right decision. It's best for everyone. Now, you must all come over and have dinner with me before I go back. Josh, would you like to come to my hotel tomorrow evening so we can all say goodbye before I go back to America?'

'Has it got a swimming pool?'

'Of course it has. Bring your swimming trunks with you and come early. I'll just go and get my things. I'm already packed.'

'Your files are in their case by the front door,' Samaya said, as she stood in the doorway. 'Your taxi is still waiting for you as you arranged.'

'Thank you so much, everybody.' Rachel quickly left.

Anita heard the sound of the taxi going down the drive. Nobody had spoken. It was almost as if a collective sigh was uttered as the three of them sat quietly on the veranda.

Josh's eyes were closing as he snuggled closer to Anita.

Dan put a hand across and squeezed Anita's. 'Josh is exhausted. We've spent the day at the elephant park. Rachel had promised to take him there but she found she couldn't fit it into her schedule so I took the day off to take him. He's already had supper at the park so I'll just put him into bed and bath him in the morning.'

'Anita, you'll come upstairs with Daddy, won't you?'

'Of course I will.'

The three of them climbed the stairs, Josh now snuggled in Dan's arms, his little arms clinging around his daddy's neck.

He fell asleep as soon as he was lowered onto his bed. Dan came round the bed and took hold of her hand, leading her towards the door. Samaya was hovering at the top of the stairs.

'My taxi has arrived, Dan, so I'll go now. See you tomorrow.'

'Yes, goodnight, Samaya. Samaya is going to spend the night at her parents' house in Rangalore,' he added as they heard the sound of the front door closing. 'So it's just the two of us now.'

He led her into his bedroom and closed the door behind them then drew her against him, kissing her gently on the lips. 'I heard some of what Rachel was saying this evening as Josh and I came through to the veranda. The rest of your heart-to-heart talk I can guess.'

'So you're psychic, are you?'

He tightened his embrace. 'No, I asked Rachel to explain her side of the story to you. A few days ago I told her about your concerns that we might get back together if she stayed. I was afraid you would leave. I asked her to explain exactly how things were between us. She said she would but she hadn't got around to it until tonight. Did she arrange to meet you here?'

'No, I'd actually come over to… Oh, well, it doesn't matter now.'

He kissed her again, this time with a deepness

of feeling that threatened to overwhelm them both. He lifted her into his arms and carried her to the bed...

The moonlight was streaming in through the window when Anita woke up. She was still in Dan's arms, her limbs languid from their love-making, her heart so full of emotion that she thought she had never felt so completely, so utterly satisfied, so deeply happy.

'Anita, there's something I've been wanting to ask you.'

She turned her head on the pillow and waited.

'I want us to spend the rest of our lives together. You know I love you, and so does Josh. We were meant to be together as a family, Anita. Will you marry me?'

She pretended to be giving some thought to the momentous question but couldn't spin out the agony of waiting any longer.

'I thought you'd never ask. I'd love to.'

Her eyes were drawn towards the window where the moon was shining in. A tapestry of twinkling stars surrounded it like diamonds arranged on a background of dark blue velvet. And just before she closed her eyes to melt into Dan's ecstatic embrace she was sure the man in the moon was looking down and giving his blessing to the new adventure they were starting out on together.

EPILOGUE

THE little boy crept quietly into his parents' bedroom. Dan and Anita were wide awake. Anita was feeding Catherine—as usual! She was always feeding Catherine, thought Josh. For a tiny six-week-old baby she seemed to need an awful lot of feeding!

'Daddy!' Josh leapt onto the bed and gave Dan an exuberant kiss. He leaned more gently across the bed so as not to harm his little sister and kissed Anita.

'Shall I kiss Catherine, Mummy?'

Anita looked down at the hungry little rosebud mouth sucking furiously at her breast. 'Better wait till she's finished feeding, Josh. You know what she's like. She might start wailing again.'

'And we had enough of that in the night,' Dan

said, leaning across to kiss his wife gently on the lips. 'Good morning, darling. Happy anniversary!'

'Happy anniversary, Dan!'

'What's an anniversary, Daddy?'

Dan propped himself up on his pillows, an arm around Josh to prevent him falling out of the crowded bed.

'Well, it's a celebration of the fact that your mummy and I have been married for a whole year. You remember the wedding last year, don't you?'

Josh smiled. 'That was brilliant. Fantastic cake and ice cream!'

'Absolutely!' Dan said, giving his son a wry grin. 'And what else do you remember?'

'Oh…everything! I remember we were in that church in the middle of Rangalore and loads of friends came from the hospital and England. Oh, and Grandma and Grandpa came from Australia.'

He looked across at Anita with a fond expression. 'And I thought that Mummy looked like a princess in that floaty white dress—everybody said so! And after you'd been weddinged—

married, isn't it?—I asked Mummy… Well, she was still Anita then. Anyway, I asked her if she would be my proper mummy now that she was married to my daddy and… What happened then, Mum? Didn't you say you had to make a phone call or something?'

'I wanted to phone Rachel in America, and ask her if she would mind you calling me Mummy.'

'Oh, yes, now I remember,' Josh said. 'And you went off for a bit and when you came back you said it would be OK.'

Anita smiled. 'I said I would be delighted if you'd call me Mummy. I'd spoken to Rachel and she'd agreed it would be a good idea and she sent her love and wished she could have been with us on our wedding day.'

Josh looked up at Dan. 'Are you going into hospital to cut people up today?'

'Not on my anniversary! I've taken the whole day off to be with my lovely family.'

Josh wriggled free of Dan's arm and climbed out of bed. 'And it's Saturday so I'm not going to school. And Mummy doesn't work any more so that's OK. Will you ever go back to the hospital to work?'

Anita, carefully moving Catherine from one breast to the other, smiled. 'When Catherine's a bit older I'll go back part time and Samaya will look after her while I'm away.'

'Samaya will like that,' Josh said. 'She says when she's looking after Catherine it makes her think of when I was a baby. She loves babies, doesn't she?'

'We all love babies,' Dan said, swinging his legs over the side of the bed.

'Well, can we have a boy baby next time, please?'

'We've got a fifty per cent chance of a boy,' Dan said. 'But I'll be happy whatever it is. Now, I'm going to go and shower and then, after breakfast, we're all going to the beach.'

'Fantastic!' Josh clapped his hands together. 'Even Catherine?'

'Of course! We'll go early before the sun gets too hot.' He paused, his eyes locking with Anita's. 'And then we'll come back home and have a siesta.'

'Now that I'm nearly seven I don't need a siesta,' Josh said importantly. 'So…'

'I've thought about that, too,' Dan said. 'Samaya is going to take you to the elephant park. They've got an indoor exercise area that's fully air-conditioned. You can feed the elephants, have a ride…'

'I remember you taking me there, Daddy! It's fab. We could take Catherine and put her on an elephant. I'll make sure she doesn't fall off, Mum!'

'I think she's better off with Daddy and me at home,' Anita said carefully. 'She sleeps very well in the afternoon.'

'That's what I'm hoping,' Dan said huskily, walking round to perch on the side of the bed close to his wife.

'I'm going to get ready!' Josh called impatiently from the landing. 'I think we should all get a move on!'

Dan bent down, his arm around Anita's shoulders as he kissed her gently on the lips.

'Later,' Anita whispered against his lips.

He raised his head. 'Promise?'

She smiled. 'Promise.'

'I love you more than I did a year ago, if that's possible, and next year I'll love you more than I do now, and the year after that I'll—'

'I love you too, but you'd better go and take that shower while I finish this feed.'

He stood up. 'This afternoon when Catherine's asleep…'

She felt her body stirring with desire again as she looked up into his eyes. All her dreams of what it would be like to live together hadn't done the reality justice. She didn't know what she'd done to deserve this perfect life, finally with the man she loved and her beautiful family, but she had certainly learned how to live each moment as if it were her last.

MEDICAL™

Large Print

Titles for the next six months…

January

VIRGIN MIDWIFE, PLAYBOY DOCTOR — Margaret McDonagh

THE REBEL DOCTOR'S BRIDE — Sarah Morgan

THE SURGEON'S SECRET BABY WISH — Laura Iding

PROPOSING TO THE CHILDREN'S DOCTOR — Joanna Neil

EMERGENCY: WIFE NEEDED — Emily Forbes

ITALIAN DOCTOR, FULL-TIME FATHER — Dianne Drake

February

THEIR MIRACLE BABY — Caroline Anderson

THE CHILDREN'S DOCTOR AND THE SINGLE MUM — Lilian Darcy

THE SPANISH DOCTOR'S LOVE-CHILD — Kate Hardy

PREGNANT NURSE, NEW-FOUND FAMILY — Lynne Marshall

HER VERY SPECIAL BOSS — Anne Fraser

THE GP'S MARRIAGE WISH — Judy Campbell

March

SHEIKH SURGEON CLAIMS HIS BRIDE — Josie Metcalfe

A PROPOSAL WORTH WAITING FOR — Lilian Darcy

A DOCTOR, A NURSE: A LITTLE MIRACLE — Carol Marinelli

TOP-NOTCH SURGEON, PREGNANT NURSE — Amy Andrews

A MOTHER FOR HIS SON — Gill Sanderson

THE PLAYBOY DOCTOR'S MARRIAGE PROPOSAL — Fiona Lowe

MILLS & BOON™
Pure reading pleasure™

1208 LP 2P P1 Medical